DOG DAYS OF CHRISTMAS

ELLE JAMES

DOG DAYS OF CHRISTMAS

BROTHERHOOD PROTECTORS BOOK #16

ELLE JAMES

New York Times & USA Today
Bestselling Author

Dedicated to the dogs who serve our country and the brave men and women who do so as well.
To my dogs, both present and past. I loved them all dearly and wish they lived forever.

Elle James

AUTHOR'S NOTE

Enjoy other military books by Elle James

Brotherhood Protectors Colorado
SEAL Salvation (#1)
Rocky Mountain Rescue (#2)
Ranger Redemption (#3)
Tactical Takeover (#4)

Delta Force Strong
Ivy's Delta (Delta Force 3 Crossover)
Breaking Silence (#1)
Breaking Rules (#2)
Breaking Away (#3)
Breaking Free (#4)

Visit ellejames.com for titles and release dates
For hot cowboys, visit her alter ego Myla Jackson
at mylajackson.com
and join Elle James's Newsletter at
https://ellejames.com/contact/

CHAPTER 1

MOLLY GREENBRIAR STOOD at the window in the maternity ward at the Bozeman hospital, staring at the baby lying in the bassinet and sighed. "He's beautiful."

Joseph "Kujo" Kuntz grunted. "Kind of red and wrinkly, if you ask me."

Molly elbowed Kujo in the belly. "That's not nice," she said. "Babies are a miracle and should be treated with respect. That little human came out of Sadie's body."

Kujo shook his head. "That, in itself, is kind of scary." He jerked a finger in the nursery's direction. "Look how big that baby is. It's hard to believe he came out of his mother. Sadie's not a big woman. She's got a small frame. How did she push that kid out?"

Molly laughed. "A woman's body is built to adjust to allow the baby to pass through. I'm sure it hurts like hell, but the result is well worth it."

Kujo's forehead creased. "Are you sure you want to have a baby? That's almost like asking for pain. Like me asking for someone to shoot me in the gut."

She gave him a twisted smile. "Not helping, Joseph. Not helping." She looked at the little boy swaddled in the hospital receiving blanket, wearing a blue knit beanie. The card tucked into the slot in his bassinet read "Baby Boy Patterson."

Molly sighed again. "What if we can't get pregnant?" she asked. "Have you thought about that?"

Kujo shrugged. "We have Six. He's turning into nothing but a big ol' baby."

She smiled. "He is a big baby of a German Shepherd, isn't he? But he's getting old. He's not going to be around forever. We've got three, maybe four more years with Six."

Kujo's frown deepened. "That dog's going to last forever. He's got nine lives, like a cat. He'll probably outlast all of us."

Molly shook her head. "On average, German Shepherds live to be between nine and thirteen years old. Fourteen, if they're lucky and stay healthy throughout their lives. Six is nine now, and he was wounded in the war."

"But he's getting the best treatment now," Kujo argued.

"Yes, but that won't help him to outlive us." Her brow wrinkled. "Don't you want children?"

Kujo slipped his arm around Molly. "You know I do. But if we don't have kids, I have you. You're all I really need."

She leaned into him. "Even with my career in the FBI, somewhere down the line, I've always imagined having a home, a husband and two-point-five children like everyone else in the country." She smiled wistfully. "When I married you, I imagined having a little girl with black hair and ice blue eyes."

He shook his head. "No, she'd look like you, with your red hair and green eyes. A little spitfire, just like her mama."

"Or a strapping boy with your broad shoulders and brooding eyebrows. Someone you could toss a football with or teach how to train dogs. Couldn't you just see two little children playing with Six? We might even get a puppy for them to play with."

Kujo drew in a deep breath and let it out slowly. "We've been trying for six months. You'd think by now something would've taken."

"Yeah," Molly said, her gaze on Baby Patterson. "I had hoped that by the annual Brotherhood Protectors' Christmas Party at the Pattersons' house, I could announce that I was pregnant. Now, I'm pretty sure that isn't going to happen. I doubt seriously that we'll even have the Christmas party since Sadie's had her baby a couple weeks early. Hank's not going to want a bunch of people in his house with a new baby there and Sadie recovering from childbirth. Nor is Sadie going to feel like organizing and hosting a party. She'll be tired and up all hours, feeding and taking care of an infant."

"Again," Kujo said, "why is it you want to have a baby?"

She slapped his arm playfully. "You know why. I want to have your baby. I want us to be a family."

"We are a family."

"I know," she said. "Six is our fur baby. But I'd like a human baby, too."

Kujo cocked an eyebrow. "Even if it is wrinkly and red?"

"I promise you, when our baby comes, you'll be proud, even if it's purple and polka-dotted because it will be ours."

"Hey, you two," a voice said behind them.

Molly and Kujo turned to find Hank Patterson standing behind them with his three-year-old daughter, Emma, in his arms. Beside him was a tall, quiet cowboy Molly recognized as Sadie's brother, Fin McClain. He carried a huge bouquet of white roses, a balloon that said *Congratulations* and a teddy bear dressed in a pale blue shirt that read, *It's a Boy.*

Kujo held out his hand. "Congratulations, old man, on another successful mission and baby number two."

Hank shook the proffered hand and nodded. "I always thought the physical demands on a body were pretty tough for Navy SEALs, but after seeing Sadie give birth to two children, I gotta say, BUD/S training pain ain't nothin' compared to giving birth."

Kujo turned to Molly. "See? You heard the boss. Why would a woman want to have a baby?"

Hank chuckled. "Beats the heck out of me. If

men were the ones responsible for giving birth, it would be the end of the human race."

Molly shook her head. "You guys are too much. A woman's body is made for this. And our hormones fake us into thinking we want this—that there's nothing better in the world than holding your own baby in your arms." She glanced back at Baby Boy Patterson. "He's beautiful, Hank. Have you chosen a name?"

"Not yet," Hank said, staring at his son. "We're still thinking about it. Before he was born, we'd narrowed the list down to about five names."

"Which names did you like most?" Molly asked.

"I liked Krull the Warrior King, but Sadie nixed that. We came up with Chase, Ledger, Matt, Dakota and Tate." Hank grinned. "All I know is that he needs a strong name. He's going to have a big sister who beats up on him all the time. He needs to be a badass to handle that." Hank kissed his daughter's cherubic cheek. "Isn't that right, Emma?"

"Emma?" Molly raised an eyebrow. "She's one of the sweetest baby girls a daddy could want." Molly touched the little girl's arm. "She's an angel."

"Yeah, but she's got three years on him now. That little boy is going to take all of her mama's attention for a while."

"You think she'll be jealous?" Molly asked.

"It's a distinct possibility," Hank said. "Hell, I'm a little jealous of the little guy. I barely get any of Sadie's attention now." He winked.

"You could name him Hank Jr.," Kujo said.

"I wouldn't wish that on any kid of mine," Hank said. "He deserves a name of his own, not to share mine."

Four other men and four women exited the elevator, laughing, and joined them in front of the nursery window.

"Good for Sadie for delivering a healthy baby boy three weeks early," Alex "Swede" Svenson said.

"How's she holding up?" Swede's girl, Allie, asked.

"She promised she'd make it through the holidays before she delivered," Swede said. "What happened?" He winked at Hank.

"He's my boy." Hank's chest puffed out. "Eager to get out of tight places and spread his wings."

"Guess that means the holiday party's off,"

Alex "Taz" Davila shook his head. "We were all looking forward to it."

His girl, Hannah, raised her hand. "Don't get us wrong. We just love getting together with rest of the Brotherhood. With the party only seven days out, we wouldn't want Sadie to go to all that trouble after just having a baby."

Hank frowned. "I'll talk with her. Maybe we can have it at a location other than the ranch."

"We could all make it happen and take the burden off Sadie," Molly offered. "She does so much already. We'd love to pull it together for her."

"Again, let me speak with Sadie. Sadie loves Christmas. She plans so far ahead, she might have the entire party set, and I don't know about it." He grinned. "She's been humming Christmas tunes since Halloween and had the Christmas decorations up on Thanksgiving Day. That's how she rolls. A baby won't slow her down." He looked from Kujo to Molly. "When are you two going to have children of your own? I thought you were planning on having a kid soon."

Kujo's jaw tightened. "Some plans don't work out, no matter how much you try."

"Still not pregnant, huh?" Hank touched Molly's shoulder. "Sorry to hear that. I've heard of people who've tried and tried to have a baby. When they finally give up, it happens."

"I'm sure that will be how it happens for us," Kujo said.

"You're not giving up yet, are you?"

"Not yet," Molly said.

"We're still willing to keep trying the old-fashioned way," Kujo said. "The next step would be to have my little swimmers tested to see if I'm shooting blanks. And I'd rather have my finger-nails pulled out than to produce a specimen in a cup."

"It could be me. My eggs might not be good," Molly said, wrinkling her nose. "We just don't know why it isn't happening."

"I'm sure it's only a matter of time." Hank shifted Emma on his arm. "Ready to go see Mommy?"

The nurse in the nursery had just changed Baby Patterson, returned him to his bassinet and rolled the cart to the door.

"That's our cue," Hank said. "We're going to see Sadie." He turned to Kujo and Molly. "You know if the stress is getting to you and it's keeping you from getting pregnant, you can always use the hunting cabin in the Crazy Mountains just to get away from the TV, internet and telephone. Sometimes, all you need is a place to go relax and get to know each other again. The key to the cabin is located underneath the flowerpot on the front porch. You're welcome to use it anytime. I'm sure Six would enjoy a romp in the snow up there, too."

Molly tilted her head, considering. "Is the cabin even accessible at this time of the year? It's been snowing up in the mountains."

"I've been up there after one of the major blizzards of the year. With the right truck, you can get there." Hank tipped his head toward Kujo. "Kujo's truck will make it up there. Anyway, it's a thought. Now, I've got to go see my beautiful wife who has given me two beautiful children. This will be the first time Emma gets to hold the baby."

Fin stepped ahead of Hank. "Let me go in before you and Emma. I want to congratulate my sister and give her these." He held up the bouquet. "I'll only be a moment."

"Sure." Hank gave Fin a head start, and then followed him down the hallway to Sadie's room.

Kujo and Molly didn't want to disturb Sadie, Hank and Emma's joyous bonding with Baby Boy Patterson. They left the hospital and drove away in Kujo's truck.

Molly turned to Kujo. "What do you think about Hank's offer?"

"What offer?" Kujo asked.

"Weren't you listening?" Molly shook her head. "He offered to let us use the hunting cabin in the mountains as a getaway. I have the next three weeks off for vacation from my job, and you don't have another assignment with the Brotherhood until the middle of January. Why don't we do it?"

He glanced her way. "Just going up to relax?"

She nodded.

"Not going to be monitoring your ovulation cycle?" he asked.

She shook her head. "Not once."

Kujo raised his eyebrows. "We're not going to obsess over getting pregnant the entire time we're up there?"

Molly sighed. "No. I'm kind of tired of the whole process."

"Although I'm a stud," Kujo puffed out his chest, "sometimes, it's hard to perform on demand."

She laughed out loud. "Like it's ever hard for you to perform on demand."

"True," he said with a grin. "But it does take some of the fun out of it."

She laid her hand on his arm. "I'm sorry."

He shook his head. "Sweetheart, don't be. I want this baby as much as you do. But if it doesn't happen, I'll be all right. I'm just worried about you."

"Well, if we can't get pregnant," Molly smiled brightly, "we can always adopt more retired working military dogs like Six."

"He does seem a little bit restless lately," Kujo remarked.

"Did you notice that his limp has practically gone away?"

Kujo smiled. "Yes, I have, and I'm happy for him."

Molly glanced at him. "So, we're doing it?"

Kujo grinned. "Looks like we're going to the mountain cabin."

Smiling broadly, Molly clapped her hands. "Good. I'm looking forward to it." Maybe at the cabin, they could get some rest, and maybe get back some of their lusty mojo that had gone by the wayside with the push to make a baby.

When they arrived at their home, Kujo helped Molly down from the truck. She hurried inside to pack clothing and blankets for their stay in the cabin. She might be overpacking, but they needed enough supplies to stay a week in the mountains. In a basket, she packed sheets, down-filled comforters, towels and washcloths and a couple of candles for ambiance and light.

The cabin had no electricity or running water. For baths, they bathed in a nearby stream in the summer. In the winter, they'd have to heat water from melting snow. It would take a lot of time to heat enough water over the open fireplace to fill the large metal washtub. For the most part, spit baths would have to do.

Six greeted them at the door, tail wagging in a somewhat subdued manner.

"Is it me, or is Six depressed?" Molly asked.

"I don't know what's wrong with him," Kujo said. "But maybe we need to take him to a veterinarian before we go out to the mountain."

Molly tilted her head. "Or maybe the mountain is just what he needs. If he gets worse, we can bring him back down."

"He definitely hasn't been himself lately."

"Do you think he's lonely?" Molly asked.

"He used to be in a kennel with dozens of other military working dogs." His eyes narrowed.

Molly's brows knit. "Do you think he's missing other dogs?"

"He's been with me for over a year," Kujo said.

Molly's lips tightened. "And with me almost as long."

"We're his pack now."

"Well, I think he's sad."

He glanced sideways at her. "You think we need to get another dog to keep him company?"

Molly's lips turned up on the corners. "Is that what you'd like me to get you for Christmas? A playmate for Six?"

Kujo shook his head. "I'm not much into Christmas. If a playmate is what will make Six happy, I don't see a need to attach it to Christmas." He glanced at Molly. "Don't get me wrong. I want Six to be happy. But why wait until Christmas?" He went back inside and came out with a bag of dog food, Six's dog bed and several chew toys.

Molly smiled. "I feel like those couples with small children. They pack everything and the kitchen sink."

"For now, Six is our baby," Kujo said.

"And he'll always be," Molly said. "He means as much to me as he does to you." Maybe they didn't need a baby to be happy…

CHAPTER 2

"SPEAKING OF CHRISTMAS…" Kujo cleared his throat as he emerged from their house, carrying a suitcase.

Molly laughed. "Were we speaking of Christmas?"

"Earlier," Kujo said. "If you want me to get something for you for Christmas, tell me what it is. Please don't make me guess."

"Not a thing." Molly patted his face. "I have everything I want in you."

His lips thinned, and he frowned. "Now you're scaring me."

"No, really. I have everything I want in you." She leaned up on her toes and brushed a kiss across his lips. There was one thing she wanted for Christmas. So far, he hadn't given it to her.

A baby.

Not from lack of trying and being a good sport about it while they'd been attempting to get pregnant. What had been amazing sex early on in their relationship had become a chore, trying to catch every ovulation cycle. They really needed to stop trying.

This trip to the mountains was a chance to get away from everything. If they didn't have a baby...oh well.

They had each other, and they had Six.

Kujo packed a bag of groceries for them and a couple of steaks for Six. Before long, they were loaded up in the truck and heading into the mountains. As Kujo drove, he shot glances in Molly's direction.

She caught him looking and smiled. "Seriously, I don't need anything for Christmas. I have everything I need in you and Six." She scratched behind the dog's ears.

Six leaned into her hand as she scratched.

"Molly," Kujo said, "you need to let me know what you want for Christmas. I've heard that when a woman says *don't get me anything*, it's code for, *Get me something good...really good.*"

Molly's eyes widened. "That's just not true."

"No?" He stared at her sitting with her arms crossed. "Then what is it you really want? A new gun, a grill for your pickup?" He raised his hands, palms up. "Give this dog a bone. I have no idea what you might like."

"I'm serious," she said. "I don't need anything. I can get anything I want, when I want." She shrugged. "I have what I need. And that's you."

"If I could give you that baby you want," he said, "I'd give it to you today."

Her eyes narrowed. "You always say the baby *I* want. What about you? Don't you want a baby, too?"

He reached out and took her hand. "Sweetheart, I'd be over the moon happy to make a baby with you, to be a daddy to a child...to *our* child. But, if it doesn't happen, I'm like you...you're all I need."

She gave him a weak smile, tears welling in her eyes. "Me and Six."

He laughed. "You and Six."

"What about adoption?" Molly asked, her

gaze going to the front windshield. "How do you feel about adoption?"

He tilted his head to the left. "I feel like there are a lot of kids out there who need a steady homelife, a pair of parents who could love them unconditionally and will look out for their welfare, education and happiness. Yes, I would be open to adoption. Even for older children who've been lost in the system."

"You don't have to worry about me loving you any less if we add a child to our home." Molly turned toward him, a soft smile on her lips. "I have enough love in my heart for you and a dozen children."

He snorted. "Did I say I was worried?"

"No," she said and squeezed his hand. "But there are some men who are jealous of the time a woman spends with a child or children that they father. And there are some women who focus all their attention on the children, with nothing left to give to their husbands." She raised his hand to press a kiss to his fingertips. "I promise that once we have a child, I won't forget you. You're the other half of me. You're who makes me complete."

"I want a child...more than one. I also know

children eventually grow up and move out," he reminded her.

Molly nodded. "Exactly. And it will be you and me again. I'm okay with that. More than okay. You're a special human, a man with a big heart beneath that gruff exterior. You're my best friend, my lover and the man I plan to grow old with. I can't imagine spending my life with anyone else but you."

He glanced toward her, his gaze capturing hers. "Good. Because I feel the same."

He turned off the main highway and drove along a gravel road that led up into the mountains, climbing higher until they were in the snow line. Though it had snowed recently, the lower elevations had already melted. They encountered patches of the white stuff in low spots, where the trees shaded it from the sun's rays. The higher they went, the less the snow had melted until they were traveling through a white winter wonderland. Another turn off the wide gravel lane took them onto a one-lane path, marked on either side by flags that indicated either side of the path. The fir trees were closer to the sides of the road, forming a tunnel of darkness.

When they finally emerged into a clearing, Kujo felt that familiar rush of relief at the sight of the hunting cabin, normally used in the fall before the snows cut it off from civilization. As he pulled up in front of the building, he looked around, a frown tugging at his brow. "I hope we don't get a blizzard up here."

Molly grinned. "If we do, we can weather it together."

"Seriously. If one of us gets hurt, a blizzard would make it impossible to get help." His frown deepened as he came to a stop in front of the small cabin where they were supposed to stay for a week. "Maybe it's not such a good idea to stay here."

Molly touched his arm. "We'll be fine. It'll do us good to stay for a week and spend time together, reminding each other why we love each other so much."

The cabin sat on the side of a hill, over-looking the valley far below where the town of Eagle Rock resided.

Kujo shifted into park and sighed, already feeling himself relax. "This will be nice, but I need to be back in town in time to get you something for Christmas. So, we'd better not get snowed in."

Molly laughed. "Hank said your truck can make it out just fine."

"You still need to tell me what you'd like." He slipped out of the truck and rounded to the other side to help her down to stand in the snow.

"Make it a surprise," she said and wrapped her arms around his neck. "I love you, babe." Then she kissed him, taking his breath away.

How had he lucked into having such a wonderful woman choose him?

Kujo hated Christmas. The stress was terrible. What did a man get the woman he loved that would show just how much he loved her?

Molly wasn't the type of woman who liked to wear fancy jewelry, or he could've gotten her some nice earrings, a necklace or bracelet. She didn't eat a lot of chocolate, and she had an aversion to roses because they drooped so quickly, reminding her that they had been cut instead of growing freely. Besides, those were something a man gave on Valentine's Day. She needed something meaningful for Christmas.

She was really sad about not being pregnant yet.

Kujo wished he could give her that one thing that would make her the happiest. A baby. So far, they'd had no luck. She'd cried the last time she'd gotten her period. Her tears had tugged at his heart. Molly never cried about anything. She was one of the strongest women Kujo knew. She had to be in order to do her job as an FBI agent. Agents didn't cry.

Whatever he did for Christmas, it had better be good. He needed to cheer her up.

He glanced into the backseat of his truck at Six, whose head overhung the two front seats. He was panting in the chill air. He'd love being in the higher altitude with the snow.

If they couldn't have a baby human, maybe Molly would like a puppy to fill that void. A puppy might make Six happy as well. He'd read that older dogs lived longer when they had a puppy to keep them company and make them feel young again.

Kujo grinned. More than likely a puppy would annoy the crap out of the old German Shepherd. Six had been an excellent military working dog, dedicating his young life to sniffing out bombs to save the troops. Now that he was retired, he deserved a good life filled with love, good food and happiness. Kujo had promised all of that to him when he'd brought Six home from the kennel at Lackland Air Force Base.

But Molly was right. Lately, Six had been a little down in the mouth and droopy. Kujo hoped the trip out to the mountain cabin would cheer up the Shepherd. He opened the back door. "Come, Six."

The dog didn't hesitate. He jumped out of the back of the truck, landing in the snow. Immediately, he pressed his nose to the snow, sniffing the ground and around the truck, moving toward the cabin. His step seemed a little lighter, and his tail lifted high. Yeah, coming to the cabin had been the right thing for Six.

Kujo stood beside Molly, starring at the little cabin. Her arm encircled his waist, and she pressed her body to his. He glanced down at her. "I'm glad we came."

She smiled into his eyes. "Me, too."

They carried their groceries, blankets and clothes into the cabin, making several trips. When they'd gotten it all inside, Kujo took Molly's hand and led her back out to witness the sunset over the top of the ridge behind them.

Then he kissed her again and walked through the door. "Come, Six."

As Six trotted toward them, a lonely wolf's howl echoed against the peaks.

Six's ears perked to attention, and he stopped dead in his tracks just outside the door.

Kujo tensed. "Six, come."

The wolf howled again.

Six lifted his snout to the sky and answered in a primal howl that echoed the wild one.

"Come, Six," Kujo repeated, his tone commanding.

Six lowered his head and turned toward Kujo. Then he looked toward the hills surrounding them. He hesitated, something he hadn't done in a very long time. The dog had been one of his best trained animals when Kujo had been on active duty. But the howl he gave was so visceral and wild, he could've been one with the wolf.

Taking a step forward, Kujo snagged the lead from the bag of dog food, snacks and bowls.

He didn't have to snap the leash on Six's collar.

The German Shepherd trotted into the cabin and waited for Kujo to close the door. Then he laid in front of the door as if to provide protection for his master.

Kujo let out the breath he hadn't realized he'd been holding.

Molly came to stand beside him, staring down at the dog. "You thought he'd go in search of the wolf, didn't you?"

Kujo nodded. "He's never hesitated performing a command."

"Maybe he was warning the wolf to stay away." Molly tipped her head toward the door. "I think he's protecting us."

Kujo's eyes narrowed. "I hope that's the case."

Together, Kujo and Molly unpacked their staples, shook out the thin mattress on the narrow bed and made it up with sheets, a down-filled comforter and the pillows they'd brought with them. After the cabin was set to rights, Kujo went out to collect the wood stacked neatly at the back of the building. Within minutes, he had a cozy fire burning in the pot-bellied stove and a pan of stew filling the air with its rich aroma.

He poured food into Six's bowl, added some of the soup on top and set it in front of the dog.

Six stood, sniffed and turned away.

"I think you're right," Kujo said to Molly.

"He's never turned up his nose at stew. If he doesn't get better, I'll take him to the veterinarian when we get back down the mountain."

"Good. I hate to think he's not feeling well." She bent to scratch the dog behind his ears. He leaned into her hand, as he usually did. He liked Molly and protected her as if she were part of his pack.

Kujo and Molly ate their meal sitting on a bench at the rough-hewn table. After they'd finished, Kujo went outside to scoop up snow in a pan and brought it back in to melt and heat over the stove to wash their dishes. He and Molly worked side by side, purposely bumping into each other. He loved when they touched and couldn't wait to get naked in the bed with her.

Once the last dish was dried, he turned, plucked the towel from her hand, hung it on a hook on the wall and pulled her into his arms. "No television, no internet, no radio..." He kissed her forehead, her cheeks and nibbled at her ear. "What else is there to do?"

She laughed. "If you don't know, we just might be doomed."

He bent, scooped her up into his arms and carried her the short distance to the bed. Then he set her on her feet and removed her clothing, one item at a time.

She worked on his buttons, his shirt, his jeans at the same time, their arms getting tangled as they raced to be free of their clothing and boots.

Once they were naked, Kujo stood back and admired his woman in the soft light of the lantern they'd lit to illuminate the small space.

Molly's pale skin glowed in the shadows, her breasts smooth, rounded globes, the swell of her hips calling to him. He reached out to pull her against him, his staff nudging her belly. He was anxious to be inside her.

However, he wanted her to be just as ready as he was to make love. He wanted her to come with as much passion and abandon as he felt in that moment. Lifting her up in his arms, he laid her across the bed, letting her legs drop over the side. He parted them with his hands, trailing his fingers up her inner thighs to the soft mound of hair hiding her sex.

Molly moaned. "Foreplay is overrated," she said. "I want you, Joseph. Now."

He chuckled. "I want you, too. But I want you to come apart at my touch."

"Sweetheart, it won't take much. I'm so

ready." She shifted her legs wider. He could see her glistening entrance. She was ready, but not as ready as he wanted her to be.

Kujo leaned over her and kissed her mouth hard and long, thrusting his tongue past her teeth to claim hers in a long gentle glide that left her breathless and wanting so much more. He trailed his mouth along the line of her jaw and down the long column of her throat to the pulse beating wildly at the base.

He touched his tongue there, feeling the beat of her heart in that moment. It was wild and primitive, like the howl of the wolf outside the cabin. His pulse hammering through his veins, Kujo swept downward as he conquered every inch of her breasts, her torso and the tight muscles of her abs, until he reached the triangle of hair at the apex of her thighs.

He knelt on the cool wooden planks of the cabin floor, letting the cold on his knees slow his own desire, ever so slightly. To bring her to the brink, he had to hold back his own urge to drive into her hard and deep. That would come…after her release.

With his thumbs, he parted the hair and folds, exposing her clit to his gaze. That narrow sliver of flesh, that nubbin of tightly-packed nerves, was the key to her pleasure, and he intended to unlock it.

He dipped his finger into her wet channel and swirled it around.

She moaned, her hips rising off the mattress. "Oh, Joseph."

He chuckled. She only called him Joseph when they were making love. He liked that. With his wet finger, he touched her clit and swirled around it, flicking and teasing it until she writhed against the comforter, her hands bunching the fabric in a tight grip.

When he thought she might be close, he touched her there with the tip of his tongue.

She tensed, drawing in a sharp breath. "Yes," she whispered, "there…"

He tapped that nubbin, gently at first, then with the sense of urgency he was feeling himself, swirling, flicking and laving until she cried out.

Molly dug her hands into his hair and held him close while her body rocked with her release. He continued licking and swirling her clit until she fell back against the pillow, her body still.

For a moment, her body lay limp against the

mattress, but then her hands again tightened in his hair, tugging.

He answered her call, climbing up her body until he leaned over her his gaze on her eyes, her face, her mouth. When he kissed her, she kissed him back, her hands gliding down over his buttocks, guiding him to her entrance.

"This is how making love is supposed to be," Molly whispered. "Wild, primitive and spontaneous. Not every move calculated to my ovulation cycle."

"Yes." Kujo growled low in his chest, feeling every bit of the passion that had been missing and loving Molly, even more.

An echoing growl sounded from the floor nearby.

Molly laughed. "Six agrees."

The dog scratched the door.

"I think he needs to go out," Molly said.

Kujo kissed her neck, her cheek and her lips. "I don't want to leave you," he said, his breath mingling with hers.

Six scratched again.

Molly captured Kujo's face between her palms. "I'll be here when you get back."

With a sigh and one more kiss, Kujo left their

bed and padded naked to the door and pulled it open.

"Use the lead—" Molly started to say.

Before he could snap the leash onto Six's collar, the dog darted through the door and out into the night.

"Six, come," Kujo said, using his dog handler's stern tone.

When Six didn't respond, Kujo repeated his command.

Again, Six didn't return. In fact, Kujo couldn't hear even the sound of the dog's paws moving in the underbrush.

Swearing softly, he returned to the bed, snatched his jeans from the floor and shoved his legs into them.

Molly rose from the bed and dressed as well. "I'm worried about Six. He might go after that wolf."

Kujo didn't say it, but he was equally worried and could have kicked himself for not snapping on the lead before opening the door. He just hadn't been thinking because his head had still been locked in the lusty euphoria of making love to Molly.

He pulled on his socks, boots and a warm winter jacket.

Molly did the same.

Grabbing his handgun, he held open the door for Molly, and they stepped out into the cold winter night.

CHAPTER 3

MOLLY ZIPPED the opening of her winter coat all the way up to her chin as she stepped out into the cold.

"Stay close," Kujo said. "The woods are full of wolves and mountain lions."

"And they're nocturnal." Molly nodded. "Don't worry." She pulled her government-issued handgun from her pocket. "I can protect myself."

In the moonlight, Kujo's lips pressed together. "A bullet from a handgun will only make a wolf mad. It might not stop him. And wolves normally travel in packs. They don't usually attack humans unless they're cornered or feel threatened. But if a pack attacks, you might only have time to shoot one, maybe two before the others are on you."

Molly smiled. "I know. That's why I'm sticking close to you." She looked out at the bright snow that was bathed in a bluish moonlit glow. "Where do you think Six went?"

"I don't know. "Kujo frowned. "He never runs off."

"Do you think he went after the wolf?" Molly asked.

"I hope not. If it's an alpha, it will tear him to shreds. Six wouldn't know what to do. He's always been around highly trained dogs that don't normally attack each other." He drew in a deep breath and called out. "Come, Six!"

They spent the next hour combing over the area around the cabin as far out as they could go without sliding down the mountain. They saw dog tracks leading up into the rocky bluff above them but couldn't climb in the dark to follow them all the way up the mountain. When Six didn't show, bark or give any sign he was still within shouting distance, Molly slipped an arm around Kujo's waist and leaned into him, exhausted, emotionally and physically.

Six meant a lot to her. He was part of her and

Kujo's family. Six had been in battle with Kujo, saving hundreds of lives with his skills sniffing out bombs. The man and the dog had a tight bond. It was one of the things that had drawn Molly to Kujo in the first place. Hell, Six had saved her life. She'd do anything for him. And the former Army Ranger cared for Six as if he were his own child. He would defend him with his life against any foe, two or four-legged.

Molly tightened her arm around Kujo's waist. "What can we do now?"

Kujo shook his head. "I can't get a search party going. Not in the dark. They don't call these the Rocky Mountains for nothing. Searching at night any farther than we have could get one of us killed. I won't ask for help until sunrise."

"In the meantime?" Molly said softly.

Kujo looped his arm around Molly's shoulders. "We hope and pray Six comes back on his own."

Alive, Molly added in her thoughts.

For half an hour longer, they stood outside, calling for Six. It was well past midnight. Her nose, fingers and toes were starting to go numb with the cold. Molly shivered.

"Oh, babe. I'm sorry. You should be inside where it's warm."

"Six isn't inside where it's warm," she protested, though the thought of warming her hands by the potbelly stove sounded like heaven.

Kujo turned her toward the cabin and walked with her. He held open the door for her to pass through.

Warmth immediately wrapped around her.

When Kujo didn't follow her inside, she stopped and faced him. "You need to come in. It's getting colder."

He drew in a deep breath and let it out. "He's tough."

"Yes, he is," Molly agreed. "And he loves the cold weather. Remember that time he stayed outside all day in the snow when the temperature was well below freezing?"

Kujo nodded. "He was playing alone."

"He'll be okay," Molly insisted. "He's smart enough to stay safe."

"If he thinks he's protecting us, he might initiate contact with potentially dangerous animals," Kujo murmured.

"Or he might make a friend and play." Molly gave her man a calming smile. "My father always said, *Don't borrow trouble, Molls.*" She touched his arm. "He'll come back, and he's going to be okay." She took his hand and led him across the threshold into the cabin, closing the door behind them. Then, piece by piece, she removed his outer clothing, then his boots, his shirt and jeans. When he stood naked in the candlelight, he worked the clothing from her body and scooped her up into his arms.

When he laid her on the bed, he climbed up beside her, pulled the comforter up over their shoulders and held her, skin to skin.

There was nothing sexual about how they comforted each other. They held each other, sharing their body heat and a common concern over the wellbeing of the other member of their family.

Molly lay awake long into the night, holding Kujo, worried about Six. Even more, she worried about Kujo. If something happened to Six…

She must have fallen asleep in the early hours of the morning. When she woke, she lay alone in the bed. For a moment, she didn't recognize where she was. Then everything that had happened the night before came flooding back. She sat up in the bed and looked for Kujo.

The small cabin was empty, the only light coming from the glow of a fire burning in the potbelly stove and the gray light of morning edging in around the shuttered windows. Kujo must have stoked the fire and then stepped out to look again for Six.

Pulling on her boots, she finger-combed her hair and shrugged into her jacket. When she stepped outside, a frigid wind whipped her hair into her face and sent a chill down her spine. Molly hunched her shoulders and pulled the hood up on her jacket to shield her ears from frostbite.

Her gaze swept the tree line, searching for Kujo and Six. She opened her mouth to call out and closed it again as a shadow detached itself from the trees and walked toward her.

Kujo.

Molly ran into his open arms. "Any sign?"

He shook his head, the dark circles beneath his eyes evidence of his lack of sleep the night before. "I followed the pawprints up into the rocky bluff above the cabin until they disappeared."

"You should have taken me," she said. "With wolves and bear in the area, I could have had your six." She frowned up at him. "I know you're worried sick about him, but you can't risk your life as well. What you need is help searching for him."

Kujo nodded. "I thought about that. I'm going to call Hank. If some of the guys are free, I'll have them come up to help me search, now that it's daylight."

"They'll come in a heartbeat. With more people searching, we have a better chance of finding him." Molly wrapped her arms around his waist and held him close. "Right now, you need to come into the cabin and warm up."

"I could use a cup of coffee," he said, holding her against him. "Then we'll drive down to Eagle Rock where we might get some cell phone reception."

"Deal." She stared up at the gray sky that hadn't lightened any more since she'd come out of the cabin. "We need everyone on the search before it snows again."

He drew in a deep breath, slipped his arm around her and walked with her across the knoll and through the door into the warmth.

"You thaw out while I get some water boiling for the coffee," she said and hurried back out with a pan to scoop snow. The wind bit her cheeks, reminding her that she needed to wrap a scarf around her neck and face to keep from getting frostbit.

Back in the cabin, she found Kujo pacing the short distance across the floor.

"Pacing won't help find him, you know." Molly laid the pan on one of the stove's burners and watched as the snow melted into water. Soon, she had two steaming cups of instant coffee poured into mugs. "Do you want me to make some breakfast?" she asked as she handed him a mug.

"No. We can get breakfast at the diner in Eagle Rock while we're waiting for Hank and the others to gather."

"Sounds good."

Kujo lifted his mug to his lips and sipped the hot brew, staring at the door. "I hate to leave in case he comes back."

"He'll stay, if he does, won't he?" Molly frowned. "Is it possible he went home? Some dogs find their way home when they're taken away."

Kujo's eyes narrowed. "Maybe."

"When we head back to Eagle Rock, we can

swing by our place and see if he's there," Molly said.

"Good idea." He took another sip of his coffee and set it on the table. "Let's go."

Molly laid her barely touched hot coffee beside Kujo's, pulled on her gloves and jacket and followed Kujo out to his truck.

Thankfully, there had been no new snow during the night. She prayed it would hold off until the Brotherhood Protectors had a chance to comb the hills, looking for Six.

With each passing hour, the dog's disappearance broke Kujo's heart a little more. Anything that bothered Kujo bothered Molly. They had to find Six.

CHAPTER 4

Kujo drove the truck down the mountain, keeping his eyes peeled for any sign of his friend and companion. He couldn't understand what had gotten into the animal for him to take off in the middle of the night like that. Six had always responded to his commands. Always.

He worried that the dog had tangled with a wolf or bear and could be lying wounded somewhere. His foot pressed harder on the accelerator, his heart squeezing in his chest. Six had helped him through a rough time in his life. Kujo couldn't just accept that the animal had disappeared. He had to find him.

As he approached a curve in the road, he realized he was going too fast and slowed, but not soon enough. The rear end of the truck skidded sideways on the gravel.

In the seat beside him, Molly gripped the oh-shit handle near the door, her face tense.

Immediately, Kujo righted the vehicle and brought it to a temporary halt. He reached across the console to take Molly's hand. "I'm sorry. I can't let my concern over Six get to me to the point I put you in danger."

She gave him a tight smile. "Thanks. I wasn't going to say anything. I know you're worried."

"But that doesn't make it right for me to drive like an idiot." He eased off the brakes and continued down the mountain at a more reasonable pace, arriving in Eagle Rock with his truck, Molly and himself intact. As soon as he was in cell tower range, he called Hank Patterson, the founder and leader of the Brotherhood Protectors, the group of former military men and women who provided security and assistance to those in need. Between Six's unconditional devotion and Hank's job offer, the two had brought Kujo from the brink of despair to a full and satisfying life…post-military.

He glanced across the cab of the truck at Molly. The FBI agent had shown him that he could love and be loved. She made him glad he was alive and gave him hope for the future with her in it.

"Hey, Kujo." Hank's voice brought him back to his purpose.

"Hank."

"I didn't expect to hear from you for a week." Hank paused. "Wait. How'd you get reception up at the cabin?"

Kujo pulled to the side of the road and shifted into park. "I'm not at the cabin. I'm in Eagle Rock. I need your help."

"What's up?" Hank asked, all business.

"Six." Kujo drew in a deep breath and let it out. "He took off around midnight last night from the cabin and hasn't come back."

"Has he ever done anything like that before?" Hank asked.

"No, sir," Kujo said. "When we arrived at the cabin, we heard a wolf's howl. Six responded."

"He didn't try to take off then?"

"No, sir," Kujo's gaze met Molly's. "It was when I let him out to do his business. He just took off. I haven't seen him since."

"You think he went looking for the wolf?" Hank asked.

Kujo nodded. "It's possible. He might have thought he was protecting us."

"And you're thinking he might have run into trouble." Hank's words were a statement, not a question. "I can see who's available to conduct a search for Six. It'll have to be quick. The weather report predicts snow this evening."

"Any tracks he might have left will be covered," Kujo concluded.

"Right," Hank said. "Where do you want to meet?"

"The diner," Kujo said. "I'm going to run out to our house and see if he showed up there. He might have gotten confused and headed home." Kujo doubted it, but he couldn't discount the theory without verifying. "I'll be at the diner in less than thirty minutes." He ended the call, shifted into drive and turned toward the road leading out to their house in the foothills on the other side of Eagle Rock.

"I hope we find Six at home," Molly murmured.

"Me, too." He didn't tell her that he didn't expect it. What little hope she could carry was better than nothing, until her hope proved wrong.

As they neared the turnoff that led to their cozy little house in the hills, Molly sat up straighter and leaned forward.

Kujo found his gaze sweeping the sides of the narrow drive through the overhanging trees, searching the shadows for the sable-colored Shepherd. His breath caught and held as they emerged into the clearing where the house sat on a knoll, the cedar and rock siding warm and welcoming.

"Do you see him?" Molly whispered.

Kujo's chest tightened as he looked around at all of Six's favorite locations to play, sleep and investigate. Finally, he let go of the breath he'd been holding. "No."

As soon as he brought the truck to a halt, Molly leaped down and ran toward the house.

Kujo dropped to the ground and followed at a more sedate pace.

She rounded the side of the house, aiming for the backyard.

He knew she wouldn't find Six there. Had the dog been at the house, he would have come out to greet them, tail wagging.

Six wasn't at the house.

By the time Kujo rounded the corner to the

back of the house, Molly was on her way back to where he stood.

"I'm sorry," she said and walked into Kujo's arms.

"For what? I didn't expect him to be here."

"I really hoped he'd just decided to go home," she said, pressing her forehead to his chest. Then she looked up. "We need to get to the diner. The sooner we get a group of people up that mountain, the sooner we find Six." She took his hand and led him back to the truck, leaving him at the front fender to help herself into the passenger seat.

He liked that about Molly. She didn't need a man to help her in and out of the truck or any other vehicle or situation for that matter. She didn't need him.

But she chose to be with him. What she didn't know was that he needed her. She was his world. The only woman who'd ever touched him so deeply he wasn't sure he could breathe without her in his life.

He stared at her through the windshield, thanking God that Six had found her in the woods when she'd been injured. If not for Six,

Molly might have died, and Kujo might never have met the love of his life.

Kujo climbed into the truck and hurried back to town. "We have to find him."

Molly nodded. "Yes. We do."

At the diner, some of the men of the Brotherhood Protectors had arrived, including Hank.

They stood in the parking lot, waiting for Kujo and Molly.

As soon as Kujo parked, they gathered around. They were his brothers. Like family, they were there to help him through the rough times life had a way of throwing their direction. Like family, they would have his back in any situation. Like family, they would help him find a loved one, even if that loved one was four-legged. They all cared about Six like he was one of their own.

Swede stepped out of the diner carrying a bag. "I had them make up breakfast biscuits, enough for all of us." He handed the bag around, letting each member of the team grab a fully-loaded biscuit, filled with eggs, bacon and cheese.

Kujo snagged one for himself and one for Molly. "Ready?" he asked the group.

They answered as one, "Yes!"

Swede rode with Hank. Taz, Duke and Boomer loaded into Chuck Johnson's truck. The two trucks full of men followed Kujo and Molly back out to the remote cabin up on the mountain.

The clouds had lowered but hadn't dumped their heavy load of snow yet. The caravan arrived at the cabin well before noon. The team split up into pairs to conduct the search, each man carrying a weapon—some handguns, some rifles.

"We don't want to lose anyone out here. Especially with a snowstorm brewing," Hank said.

"Don't take any risks on the rocks. They'll be slick with ice or moisture. Either way, stick within sight of your buddy. Be bear aware."

"And watch for wolves," Kujo warned.

Swede distributed communications equipment, consisting of two-way radio handsets that could carry a signal for up to two miles. They tested the devices before they broke up into groups going several different directions and struck out, calling loudly for Six.

"Stick with me," Kujo told Molly. "I couldn't bear it if I lost you, too."

She hugged his arm and set off, heading up the steep slope behind the cabin. Kujo wanted to explore deeper into the rocky bluffs above, afraid Six might have fallen in the darkness. He prayed they'd find him alive.

CHAPTER 5

Molly scrambled up the side of the hill. As the slope grew steeper, she followed a little slower, using her hands and knees when she had to. She didn't dare look back behind her, afraid she'd freak out at how steep the side of the hill really was. Looking up was so much easier than looking down, even knowing they would eventually have to make it back down to the cabin.

At one point, they found pawprints in the snow. They were canine, but Molly didn't think they were Six's. "Too big for Six?" she asked

Kujo nodded. "Probably a wolf."

Molly frowned up at Kujo. "Do you think it was the one howling when we drove up yesterday?"

"Could be," he said, his lips pressed into a tight line. His hand rose to the gun he kept tucked in the pocket of his jacket. "Let's keep looking."

Her own hand patted her pocket where her handgun lay. She was an expert shot at the gun range. Would she be as skilled when it came to defending them against a wild animal?

Her jaw firmed.

Hell, yeah.

She'd do anything to protect Kujo and Six.

Her gaze swept across the rocky landscape searching for their beloved four-legged friend. Even as the clouds descended to envelop them in a hazy fog, she couldn't help thinking Six might be in trouble, possibly cold and hurt. Though visibility was getting more difficult, they couldn't give up. Not yet.

When the first snowflakes started falling, the men of the Brotherhood Protectors radioed in, reporting their status.

"If it gets worse, head back to the cabin," Hank warned. "White-out conditions up here can be deadly."

They all agreed.

Conditions worsened, the snow coming

down thicker, heavier, obliterating any chance of finding pawprints.

"Bring it in," Hank finally said. "We'll have to wait until it quits snowing before we can continue."

Kujo and Molly were the last to arrive back at the cabin.

The others stood around, stamping their feet and rubbing their hands together to keep warm.

Hank met them as they emerged from behind the building. "Good. Now that you two are here, we're all accounted for. Any signs?"

Kujo shook his head. The hollows beneath his eyes breaking Molly's heart.

"The snow could be a blessing," Hank said. "When it's finished, we'll have a blank canvas to look for more pawprints. Some of the rocky surfaces had been swept clear of all snow up until now." He glanced around at the men awaiting his next orders. "We can wait in the cabin or drive down the mountain while we can." He glanced up at the sky, snowflakes falling so hard, he blinked. "I doubt you have enough supplies on hand here to sustain us if we get snowed in."

Kujo sighed. "We need to get down from the mountain."

Molly's gaze turned to the cabin that was supposed to have been their home away from home for a week. Remote, beautiful and theirs for that short timeframe to reconnect as a couple.

Now, all she could think was that if they left and Six returned, he'd have no one waiting for him. "Kujo and I will stay here," Molly said, firmly. "Someone has to be here if—*when*—Six comes back." She swallowed hard on the lump forming in her throat. After searching all morning and well into the afternoon, finding no evidence that Six was still around, Molly couldn't help but feel doubtful. For Kujo's sake, she refused to show it. Six *would* come back. A glance at Kujo's devastated face made Molly's heart hurt. Six *had* to come back.

Hank frowned. "Are you sure you two will be okay here on your own?"

Kujo nodded. "You need to be down the mountain with your wife and new baby." He smiled. "Have you even chosen a name?"

A twisted grin spread across Hank's face. "No. Sadie wanted to get to know our little beast before she decided. They almost wouldn't let us out of the hospital without a name on the birth certificate."

"Hopefully, by the time we come down, you'll have a name to share," Molly said. "Give Sadie our love and go. You don't want to be stuck up here when your family needs you."

Kujo held out his hand. "Thanks for helping."

Hank's lips turned downward. "I'm sorry we didn't find him."

"He'll come back," Kujo said.

Molly could tell by the hollowness of Kujo's tone that the man didn't hold out much hope the dog would make it back to the cabin. If he hadn't come back by now, he most likely had been injured or killed.

Her eyes stinging, Molly slipped her hand in Kujo's and watched as the men climbed into the two trucks and headed down the mountain, the snow falling in thick, heavy flakes all around them.

As soon as the vehicles disappeared behind the white curtain of frozen precipitation, Kujo brought Molly's hand up to his lips and pressed a kiss to the back of her knuckles. "Let's go in and get warm."

She let him lead her back into the cabin where the start of their mini-vacation had been so exciting and filled with promise. Now, the inside of the cabin was more of a tomb without Six there. The higher the snow piled, the more depressed Molly became.

They stood for a long time beside the potbelly stove, warming their fingers, toes and faces.

Soon, Molly's stomach rumbled. She set a cast iron skillet on top of the stove and dropped a pat of butter on its surface. Soon, she had eggs scrambled and the biscuits she'd brought from home cooking on a skillet. They ate in silence at the little table. Twice, she moved to give Six a piece of her biscuit, as was her habit. Twice, she was reminded of the dog's absence.

Kujo's gaze followed her hand both times, his jaw tightening.

"I miss him, too," she whispered.

"You were teaching him bad habits," Kujo said, though a gentle smile curled the corners of his lips.

Molly gave him a sad smile. "He deserved a little spoiling. He served his country bravely." Her eyes misted. "When he gets back, I plan on spoiling him even more." She lifted her chin, daring Kujo to disagree.

He nodded. "Me, too. You're right. He deserves to be spoiled."

With no couch or comfortable chairs to sit in, they retired to the bed where they lay in each other's arms. Every sound had Molly's ears perking, praying it was Six scratching at the door to be let inside.

Several times, Kujo got up to check outside, letting in a cool blast of arctic air. He'd return to the bed, his hair dusted with huge white flakes of snow, his face grim.

The snowstorm lasted all through the day and into the night. Not until the following day did the clouds lift enough to let them get back out and look for Six. Molly wished Hank and his guys could have come back out to help, but the road was packed with snow, and Hank had his hands full with a new baby.

They searched all day, until their feet were freezing, and the clouds moved back in to dump more snow on them.

Molly and Kujo spent another night wrapped in each other's arms. She comforted him the only way she knew how—with her body, making love into the small hours of the morning. Still, Six didn't return.

The days drifted by until the end of the week when they were due to leave the cabin.

It was their last day at the mountain cabin. Kujo was out of the bed before Molly.

She opened her eyes to find him standing in front of the potbelly stove. She took the opportunity to study him, while he wasn't looking. God, she loved his broad shoulders and narrow waist, and the way his eyes crinkled when he grinned or laughed.

He hadn't smiled since Six had disappeared.

"Hey, you," she whispered.

He spun to face her. "You're awake."

She laughed. "Yes, I am. Unless I'm talking in my sleep."

"I have coffee." He poured hot water into two mugs, stirred in instant coffee and carried the mugs to the bed, handing one to Molly. Then he sat on the side of the bed.

Molly wrapped her hands around the warm mug. "I hate to leave."

Kujo nodded. "Me, too." He sipped his coffee, staring at the door. "It might not make a difference, but I'd like to look for Six one more time."

Molly nodded. "You know I'm perfectly okay with that. We can spend as much time as you need here, looking for Six."

His lips thinned. "We can't stay here forever. If we don't find him today, hopefully, he can find his way home."

Swallowing the lump in her throat, she took his hand. If he hadn't come back to the cabin by now, and he hadn't made it back to their home, he probably wasn't going to make it back at all. She didn't say it out loud. Molly wanted Kujo to hold on that little bit of hope for just a little longer.

She swung her feet over the side of the bed and pushed to stand on the cold, wood floor. For a moment, her vision blurred, she swayed, and her stomach churned.

Kujo steadied her with an arm around her waist. "What's wrong?"

"Nothing," she said. "I just got up too fast."

"Lean on me," he insisted.

She slipped her arm around his waist and leaned into his arm, loving the woodsy scent of the man. She wished they didn't have to leave, but they needed to return to their home. It would be Christmas soon. After the holiday,

Molly would go back to her job with the FBI. Kujo would take on another assignment with the Brotherhood Protectors.

"Better?" Kujo asked.

Molly straightened. "Better." In that moment, her stomach upended. She dove for the door, yanked it open and ran out barefoot into the snow, where she promptly emptied the contents of her belly.

Kujo was right with her, holding her hair back from her face.

When she could stand straight again, he scooped her up into his arms and carried her back inside to stand next to the stove where her hands and feet could thaw from the chill outside. When he was certain she could stand on her own, he grabbed a towel and dried her feet. Then he pulled a pair of his thick socks over her toes and heels. "I'm not going to go look for Six," he said. "I think it's time for us to get down off this mountain."

Molly shook her head. "Oh, no. I'm fine. Actually, I feel better now that I've purged my stomach."

Kujo's eyes narrowed. "I'm not leaving you here alone while I go out looking for Six."

"You're right. You're not going out looking for Six by yourself." She squared her shoulders. "I'm going with you."

"No way," Kujo said. "You almost passed out and then barfed your guts up. You're in no condition to take care of yourself." He lifted her hand. "We're taking you into town to see a doctor."

"I'm okay," she said. "Really, I am. I think I ate something wrong."

"You haven't eaten anything this morning," he pointed out.

Molly waved a hand. "Then, last night. I'm not leaving until I've looked for Six one last time."

"I'm not letting you out of this cabin to do that." Kujo crossed his arms over his chest.

"Who do you think you are?" she asked with righteous indignation.

"Just a boy taking care of a girl." He crossed to stand in front of the door.

"You can't go looking for Six on your own," she said. "You need a backup. Someone to cover your ass if you should be stalked by a wolf or a bear."

His eyebrows drew together. "You're not

going mucking around in the woods and mountains when you're feeling sick to your stomach and lightheaded. It's a recipe for disaster."

Molly blinked her eyes. "I feel fine now. In fact, I feel better than fine. I feel downright normal." She grinned. "I was only dizzy because I got up too fast. I'm up now, moving, and everything is as it should be."

Kujo's eyes narrowed as he ran his gaze over her from head to toe.

"If you don't take me with you," Molly crossed her arms over her chest, much like Kujo had, "I'll follow you, anyway. So, get over it and take me with you."

"If you faint, I'll have to carry you out over rocky ground and through the trees." He lifted his chin. "What's to keep us from falling over a cliff?"

"If we fall over a cliff, at least we'll go together," she said with a grin.

Kujo's lips quirked on the corners. "You do have a point. If we've gotta go, I'd rather we went together. Though I'd rather you didn't go at all." He tipped his head toward the food they'd brought. "You should at least eat something before we go."

Molly grabbed a handful of saltine crackers from a box on the shelf. "This will be enough to keep me going. I don't think I can handle anything else."

Kujo's eyes widened. "See? You don't feel better."

Molly sighed. "I do. Really. I just don't want to risk being sick out there. The crackers will help settle my stomach, and they'll keep me from bottoming out because I haven't eaten."

"You're a hardheaded woman," Kujo growled.

"And you're a hardheaded man."

Kujo chuckled. "It's a wonder we're still married." He gripped her arms and brought her close. "I love you so much," he said. "I don't want to lose you as well."

Molly hugged him back. "You're not going to lose me. I promise."

CHAPTER 6

THEY SPENT the next couple of hours searching for Six and not finding a single trace of his existence. No pawprints, no droppings. Nothing. It was as if he'd disappeared off the face of the earth.

The sun hit its zenith and started its descent, heading toward the mountain peaks.

Kujo and Molly returned to the cabin, packed their belongings and loaded them into the back seat of the truck.

Kujo didn't say it, but nothing felt right without Six sitting in the back seat with all their stuff, sticking his head between the two front seats to watch the road ahead. When they were ready, Kujo stood outside the cabin door, peering into the shadows of the trees and up the rock face of the mountain where he'd seen the pawprints that first night.

Molly rested her hand on his arm, without saying a single word.

Kujo took her hand and led her to the passenger side of the truck where he helped her up into the cab. Then he slipped behind the steering wheel and drove down the mountain toward the little town of Eagle Rock. As soon as they reached the edge of town and the cell phone towers, Kujo's phone beeped, indicating incoming text messages and voice mail. Several of his teammates had left messages, each of them wishing he'd had luck finding Six and to let them know as soon as he returned to town. The last message was a recording from Hank.

"Hey, Kujo and Molly. I know you won't receive this message until you get back in town. But I want you to know Sadie insisted we go ahead with the annual Christmas party at the ranch, even with the new baby. All the ladies and guys pitched in to decorate and cook the food to make it happen. We're having the party on the originally scheduled date. That's the Saturday night that you two get back to town. So, if you feel up to it, please join us. Everyone will be there, and we'd love to see you."

Kujo glanced over at Molly. "What do you think?"

Her gaze shot out the window at the street in front of them. "I don't know. I don't feel much like celebrating. We didn't find Six."

"True, but if we go home and stay at the house all evening, we'll just get more depressed because he's not there."

"I guess that means we're going to a party," Molly said, her voice wry.

Kujo didn't want to go to a party, but he couldn't face staying home when Six's dog bed and food dish would be empty. The space in Kujo's heart that Six had filled would be empty and hurting. Molly loved Six as much as he did. She'd be sad.

Christmas was the season to spend time with friends and family.

Yeah, they'd go to the party.

When they arrived at their house, it was just as he'd thought. The entire place felt wrong and depressing without Six there to greet them.

They unloaded the truck and put away the

groceries, threw their clothing into the laundry room and hurried into the shower together.

Kujo washed Molly's red hair, massaging her scalp the way that made her purr like a contented cat. He let the suds wash over her shoulders and down her body, his hands following their paths. Pulling her back against him, the hard ridge of his cock pressed against her buttocks.

Molly leaned her head back against him, resting it against his chest. "We're going to be okay, aren't we?"

He nuzzled her ear. "Yes."

"I miss Six."

"Me, too," he said, nibbling her earlobe. "But I have you."

"And I have you," she said.

"As long as we have each other, we'll be all right."

Molly turned in his arms and kissed him.

Kujo couldn't imagine what he'd have done without Molly. Six meant a lot to him. So did Molly. Though he'd lost Six, he still had Molly. He couldn't screw that up.

He made love to her, pressing her back against the cool tile wall of the shower, her legs wrapped around his waist, his staff buried deep inside her slick channel.

She laced her hands behind his neck and rode him hard.

God, he loved this woman with all of his heart.

When the water cooled, Kujo turned and switched it off. He grabbed a towel and dried every inch of her body, kissing her smooth skin along the way, enjoying the feel of her body beneath his lips.

She dried him with a fresh towel and kissed him all over. If they didn't have a party to go to, he'd have taken her to bed and made love to her all over again. Instead, they walked naked into their room and dressed.

Kujo slipped into a pair of jeans, a crisp white button-down shirt, his cowboy boots and a black leather jacket.

After Kujo finished dressing, Molly made him leave the bedroom, claiming she had an early Christmas present for him that she needed to wrap.

"I haven't gotten yours yet," he protested.

"Don't worry. This was something I've been working on for a while."

He paced the living room floor, mad at himself that he hadn't gone to the jewelry store yet to pick up the ring he'd had sized to fit her right hand. They had a few days before Christmas. He'd be able to get to the jeweler before Christmas Day and have them wrap it for her. It was an emerald ring that would go nicely with the color of her eyes.

When Molly emerged from the bedroom, she was stunning in a long, red dress that fit her body like a second skin. The fabric clung to every inch of her like it belonged. She'd pulled her red hair up into a messy bun on top of her head, exposing the long line of her neck and the curve of her shoulders.

"Wow," he said. "That's new."

She gave him a sexy smile. "I bought this as a gift for you for Christmas. I'd planned on wearing it to the Christmas party as a surprise."

"Well, I am surprised, and that dress is gorgeous." He pulled her into his arms. "Should I change into something more formal?"

She shook her head. "No, you look wonderful just the way you are." Molly wrapped her arms around his neck. "Still want to go to the party?"

"I have to admit I'm having second thoughts,

seeing you in that dress. I'm trying to think of all the different ways I can take it off of you." He drew in a deep breath and let it out slowly. "But we can't waste that dress on just me."

"Why not?" she asked.

"I have to show you off and make all of my teammates envious." He smiled down into her eyes. "Besides, the longer I have to wait to strip you out of that dress, the hotter I'll be. And I can study its design so I can make quick work of taking it off you."

She turned, showing him her back. "It's easy," she said. "It's just one short zipper in the back."

His groin tightened. The zipper was very short, extending from the small of her back to halfway over the curve of her ass, leaving most of her back naked.

"You're going to make it really hard on me, keeping my hands to myself," he said.

She chuckled. "Is the key word *hard on?*"

Kujo clutched her to him, pressing her hips to his. "Damn right." He kissed her then set her at arm's length. "Let's get there so we can get back. I'm ready to test that zipper."

Molly handed him a white leather coat. He held it open while she slipped her arms into it.

Then she cinched the belt around her waist. "I'm ready."

Kujo opened the door and stepped out onto the porch. In the back of his mind, he prayed he'd find Six lying on the decking. He'd look up at them, tail thumping the planks. However, Six wasn't there. A hard knot formed in his gut.

Kujo consoled himself with the fact he would have the prettiest girl at the party that night. He promised himself, for Molly's sake, that he wouldn't mope. He had Molly, the woman he loved. His lifeline. As long as he had her, they'd get through the loss of Six together.

They accomplished the drive out to White Oak Ranch in silence. He focused on the road ahead and Molly in her go-to-hell red dress. He wasn't sure what Molly was thinking of, but she wasn't frowning, and she didn't have a sad expression on her face. Seeing their friends, spending time talking and visiting would keep her thoughts away from the loss of Six.

At least a dozen trucks were parked in front of the rock and cedar ranch house. The porch and interior were lit up like a convention center. Someone had strung colored lights on the porch rails and posts, giving the house a festive look and feel. It was beautiful, just like it had been for the past couple of years.

"How does Sadie manage all this?" Molly asked.

Swede and his wife, Allie, met them at the front door.

"Sadie and Hank would've been here to invite you in," Allie said. "But Sadie's got the baby with her and didn't want to stand in the cold with him."

Molly shook her head. "We wouldn't have expected her to have him out in the cool night air. He's only a week old."

"Did they ever come up with a name for him?" Kujo asked.

Allie nodded. "Yes. But they haven't told anyone. They said they weren't sharing that name until we were all here." She clapped her hands. "I can't wait. And he's such a cutie. He's got his father's dark hair. And I'll bet my favorite horse he'll have Hank's signature green eyes."

Allie touched Kujo's arm. "We all know you didn't find Six. Everyone feels bad, but they promised not to talk about it and bring everyone down."

"Thank you," Kujo said. "We're still trying to come to grips with his loss."

Allie nodded. "We figure you're sad enough as it is. You don't need to be reminded."

"Thank you," Molly said. "Let's just enjoy the evening."

Kujo could see the moisture pooling in Molly's eyes. He slipped the jacket off her shoulders and handed it to Allie. Swede held out his hand for Kujo's. "We'll hang them in the hall closet. You can help yourself when you leave."

With a hand at the small of Molly's naked back, Kujo escorted her into the large living area filled with all the Brotherhood Protectors, their spouses and children. The couple made their rounds, shaking hands and greeting everyone until they came to a halt in front of a rocking chair where Sadie held a baby in her arms. Her three-year-old little girl, Emma, played at her feet with Boomer and Daphne's little girl, Maya, and Chuck and Kate's daughter, Lyla.

Molly bent to hug Sadie. "How did you pull this off after just having a baby?"

Sadie laughed and waved her hand around the room. "Everyone pitched in. I sat around and watched the masters at work."

"Don't let her fool you," Daphne said. "She did her share of directing and got it all taken care of quickly and efficiently."

"That's right," Chuck said. "Hank's bride has this down to a science."

Sadie held out a hand to Kujo. "I'm sorry about Six. I really hope that he'll find his way home."

Kujo took her hand and held it in his for a moment. "I hope he comes home soon." He held out his hand to Hank. "I hear you have an announcement to make." He grinned at his boss.

Hank cleared his throat loudly. "I do." He shook Kujo's hand and let go, turning to the others in the room. "I'm glad you all could make it to the annual Brotherhood Protectors Christmas party. Thank you for making this organization the success it is. We've grown considerably since Swede and I joined forces to make it happen. You have my undying gratitude for making this dream come alive. And you'll find an extra bonus in your paycheck."

"You don't have to thank us, Hank," Chuck said. "We should thank you for taking a bunch of military dudes and giving us a purpose in life."

"Here! Here!" the men cheered.

Hank grinned.

"The bonuses are all well and good," Taz said. "Thanks for the money. But what we really want to know is did you choose a name for Baby Patterson?"

Hank laid a hand on Sadie's shoulder. She covered it with one of hers and smiled up at him. "We did."

"Ladies and gentlemen, please meet the newest addition to the Patterson family..." he paused for a very long moment.

"Seriously, Hank," Swede said. "We're not on reality TV."

"Stop being dramatic, dear," Sadie said.

Hank heaved a sigh. "Allow a man a moment, will ya? Our baby's name is McClain Patterson."

The people in the room cheered softly so as not to disturb baby McClain.

"His mother did all the work of carrying him and giving birth. She deserved to have him named after her," Hank explained, then added with a grin, "and I get to nickname him Mac."

Kujo looked down at the baby boy. "Mac. It's a good name. And he's got a great pair of parents to raise him."

"And a big sister to torment him," Molly said with a wink.

Kujo liked when Molly teased. The light in her eyes made him want to crush her to him and kiss her all over again.

"Kujo, would you mind holding Mac? I'd like to get up." Sadie handed Mac up to Kujo.

Hank held out a hand to help her to her feet and into his arms. "I love you, Sadie McClain."

"I love you, too," she said and kissed him in front of everyone.

Kujo stood with the tiny baby in his arms, afraid to move in case he slipped and dropped the infant. "What do I do?"

Sadie laughed. "Just hold him. He's asleep."

"What if he wakes?" Kujo asked, his pulse pounding hard in his chest.

Hank chuckled. "I'm sure we'll figure it out." He clapped Kujo on the back, jolting him.

Kujo wanted to tell him to watch it.

Sadie touched Kujo's arm. "You'll make a great father, Joseph," she said with a smile.

He didn't want to tell her that they'd had no luck in that department. Hell, he didn't want to say anything that made him lose focus on the child in his arms.

Sadie nodded to Molly. "Would you mind helping me with a tray of hors d'oeuvres?"

"Just point the way. I'll get it," Molly said. "Shouldn't you be resting?"

"I'm fine," Sadie said. "I want to see what's happening in the kitchen."

Kujo watched the two women make their way to the kitchen, wishing Molly would come back and take Mac from him. The baby boy shifted, nuzzling his face against Kujo's shirt. He was so small.

And precious.

Longing built in Kujo's chest. He'd said having a baby wasn't everything. Molly meant the world to him. If they weren't able to have children, he'd be all right.

But staring down at the baby boy in his arms, he couldn't stop the emotions welling up inside him. He wanted a child. God help him.

CHAPTER 7

MOLLY FOLLOWED Sadie into the kitchen.

"Joseph looked like a natural holding Mac," Sadie murmured.

Molly laughed. "I don't think I've ever seen such a look of stark terror on a man's face."

Sadie chuckled. "Yes, but he was so gentle with him. I think he'll be good with a baby of his own."

Molly didn't respond.

Sadie popped a plate of sausage and cheese balls into the microwave for thirty seconds and turned to Molly. "So, when are you two expecting?"

Molly's eyes filled with tears. "We're not."

Sadie frowned. "What do you mean? You're practically glowing."

Molly shook her head, the scent of sausage and cheese making her stomach churn. "We're not expecting, even though we've been trying for the past six months."

The microwave dinged, indicating the thirty seconds were up. "I don't understand," Sadie said, pulling the plate out of the oven.

When Sadie turned with the loaded plate, the strong aroma of cheese and sausage wafted toward Molly. Her eyes widened, and her stomach roiled. She pressed a hand to her mouth. "I think I'm going to be sick."

Sadie set the plate on the counter and hooked Molly's arm. "Come with me." She led Molly to the bathroom in the master suite.

Molly made it just in time to lean over the commode and toss the crackers she'd eaten earlier that day.

Sadie brushed her hair back from her face and helped her to stand. "I couldn't stand the smell of bacon during my first pregnancy."

"But I'm not pregnant," Molly insisted.

"Have you taken an early pregnancy test?"

Molly nodded, stepped over to the sink,

splashed water in her face and rinsed her mouth. "A few weeks ago. It was negative. I don't think we were meant to have a baby. We've been trying so hard."

"I've seen so many of my girlfriends trying so hard, but when they finally gave up, they got pregnant." Sadie opened a cabinet door and shuffled through the contents, finally finding what she was looking for. She held out a box. "I think you need to try the test again. I had an extra from when we were trying for Mac."

Molly held up her hands. "I can't."

"Sure you can. I'm not going to need it for a while. Mac's going to keep me plenty busy."

"No. I can't. If it's negative, I'm going to lose it. I don't want to ruin the evening for Joseph by blubbering like a baby."

Sadie laid her hand on her arm. "Sweetheart, I'll be right outside the door. If you feel the need to cry, we can do it together. It'll be our secret." She took Molly's hand and placed the box in it. "I think you need to do this. Do it for me." She winked and backed out of the bathroom. "I'm right outside."

Molly stared at the box, her hand shaking so much she almost dropped it.

She told herself she'd be all right if it came back negative. It was just another test. Another disappointment, nothing as sad as losing Six. She wasn't sure she could handle another blow.

Still, she hadn't felt well all day. And it wasn't like she was really ill, just bluh.

She opened the box, pulled out the wand and carried it to the toilet. Gathering her pretty red dress in her arms, she peed on the stick and waited the recommended three minutes for the results, her heart lodged in her throat.

When she guessed the time was up, she couldn't look at the wand, couldn't bear to see the word "no" in the window. Instead of reading it, she set it on a piece of toilet paper on the counter, washed her hands and straightened her dress. Then she opened the bathroom door.

"Well?" Sadie asked, her eyes wide and excited.

"I can't."

"Can't what?" she asked. "Can't pee? Sweetheart, I can load you up with a gallon of water. We can make this work."

"No," Molly shook her head. "I can't look. I don't think I can stand to see the word NO one more time."

"You took the test, but you haven't read the results?" Sadie squeezed past her. "Where is it? Oh, here it is. I'll read it for you."

"No." Molly grabbed Sadie's arm. "I don't want to know."

"Holy hell, Molly. You may not want to know, but I'm dying here." She grabbed the stick with a dry washcloth and turned it over.

Molly spun away, her eyes filling with tears. "I don't want to know," she whispered, pressing her fingers to her ears.

Sadie touched her arm. "Molly, you need to see this for yourself."

"No. I just can't." A tear slipped from the corner of her eyes and ran down her cheek.

"Sweetie, you have to." Sadie shoved the test wand in front of her face.

Molly looked down at the window before she could look away. In the little box was the word YES. After seeing NO for the past six pregnancy tests, Molly wasn't sure she was seeing straight. "I don't understand."

"It says 'yes'!" Sadie squealed. "You're pregnant, Molly. You and Joseph are going to have a baby."

Molly's heart turned a somersault, and her vision blurred. "I'm going to have a baby?"

"Yes," Sadie said.

Molly fought the darkness but didn't win. She sank to her knees in her pretty red party dress and slumped onto the cool marble tile of the bathroom floor.

CHAPTER 8

"HERE, LET ME TAKE HIM." Hank held out his hands for his small son.

Kujo had just gotten used to the feel of the infant in his arms. But he handed the child over to his father, breathing a sigh of relief.

"Joseph," Sadie called out, standing at the edge of the living room, her brow wrinkled with worry. "I need you. ASAP."

Kujo frowned and hurried across the floor toward Hank's beautiful movie star wife. "What's wrong?"

"It's Molly. She passed out on the floor of my bathroom. I need your help to get her up into a bed."

Kujo ducked past Sadie, ran for the master bedroom and crossed to the adjoining bathroom.

Molly was sitting up on the floor, looking at a plastic stick.

"Molly, sweetheart, are you all right?" He knelt on the floor beside her and gathered her into his arms.

She nodded, tears spilling from her eyes, dotting her pretty red dress with moisture. "I'm more than all right." Her face tilted up to his and a smile spread across it, rivaling the lights shining down on her. She held up the stick.

He glanced down at it, not quite comprehending what she was trying to get across to him. "Did you hurt yourself?" He slipped his arms beneath her and lifted her off the floor. "Do I need to take you to the hospital?"

She laughed and shook her head. "Not yet. But nine months from now, you'll have to take me."

"What are you talking about? Sadie said you passed out." He looked down into her eyes. "That's the second time today you've gotten lightheaded."

Molly captured his face with one hand and looked him square in the eye. "Will you stop worrying about me and look at what I'm trying to show you?"

He looked again at the plastic stick. In a little box on the side of it was one word.

Yes

His brow wrinkled, and his gaze settled on the wand as realization hit him. "Is that what I think it is?"

Molly nodded. "It's a 'yes'."

"You're…"

"Pregnant. Yes. I'm pregnant." Molly wrapped her arm around his neck and kissed him full on the mouth. "We're going to have a baby."

"What? Wait… How?" He stumbled with his words.

A chuckle sounded from the master bedroom. "If you don't know how, there's no hope for you, Kujo," Hank said with a laugh. "Congratulations, you two. I couldn't be happier for you."

"I'm going to be a daddy," Kujo said.

Molly laughed at the wonder on her husband's face. "We're going to have a baby," she whispered.

Kujo crushed her to him, burying his face in

her neck. "I love you, Molly. More than you'll ever know."

"I love you, too, Joseph." She held him close, tears of joy wetting her face.

When he at last looked up, Kujo grinned at Hank and Sadie standing there, holding Mac. "I'm going to be a father."

"Yes, you are."

Kujo's eyes widened. "I'm going to be a father," he said, his voice shaking. "I don't know how to be a father."

"Don't worry. All you have to do is love your baby," Sadie said.

Molly laughed, so happy, she could barely breathe.

Kujo carried her out of the bedroom into the living room.

"Where are we going?" Molly asked.

"Home."

"Why?"

"You need to rest. Put your feet up. Take it easy. You're carrying a baby inside you."

Molly laughed. "It's not even the size of a peanut at this point. I don't need to rest."

"You passed out. I'd say you need to rest."

Molly laughed and looked over Kujo's

shoulder at her host and hostess. "I guess we're going home for the night. Thank you for having us. And, Sadie, thank you for the test. I owe you."

Sadie shook her head. "I'm just happy your dreams are coming true. Merry Christmas!"

Kujo didn't stop to bid goodbye to his teammates or his host. He marched out to his truck, gently deposited Molly on the front passenger seat and climbed in. They were home in record time, though Kujo drove safely.

Before Molly could get out of the truck, Kujo was around the front to her side to help her down.

For a long moment, he held her in his arms, staring down at her face in the light beaming from the inside of the truck. "I love you, Molly. So very much. And I promise to love our baby and take care of you both for as long as I live."

"Which better be a very long time." Molly stood on her toes and brushed her lips across his. "Congratulations. You're going to be a daddy."

"AND YOU'RE GOING to be a mommy." Kujo grinned so wide he thought it might split his face. He bent and scooped Molly up into arms, carrying her across the yard to the house.

As he climbed the steps, he nearly tripped on something lying in his path.

It darted out of his way and stopped a few feet away.

"Put me down," Molly said, struggling to get down.

Kujo let her legs fall to the ground and held her until she was steady on her feet.

Molly flipped the light switch for the front of the house, bathing the porch in soft yellow light.

There on the wooden deck, looking up at them with his deep brown eyes stood the most beautiful German Shepherd Kujo had ever had the privilege to work with.

"Six," he whispered and dropped to his knees in front of the dog.

Six went into his arms and rested his head against Kujo's neck, making soft whining noises.

"Are you hurt?" Kujo asked, leaning back to get a good look at the animal.

Six looked to be perfectly healthy, with no signs of injury or illness.

"How did you find your way back?" Kujo asked, hugging Six tightly. "Are you hungry?

You've been a week without food." Kujo ran his hands over the dog's body. He felt bonier, but not terribly. "Come. Let's get you some food."

Six licked his face and struggled to be free. Once he was, he leaped down from the deck and ran out into the yard.

"Six, come," Kujo said, his voice stern. Fear of losing his friend again made him go after the dog.

Molly reached out and grabbed his arm. "Don't," she said softly.

"But he might run off again." Kujo tried to shake her hand free.

Molly refused to let go. "He came back. He'll come back again," she said.

"But I don't want him to go away. He belongs here with us."

Molly nodded toward the tree line where the light from the porch cast shadows. "He's not alone."

Kujo stared into the shadows. "What do you mean?"

In the darkness, a light gray ghost of a figure moved between the trees.

Six ran out to the edge of the clearing, stopped and looked back at them on the porch.

The gray ghost of an animal moved again.

"It's a wolf," Kujo said, and he started for the steps. Again Molly held him back. "Six, come!" he called out.

"He's not afraid," Molly said.

Six ran into the shadows and met up with the gray wolf, nuzzling it with his nose.

Molly smiled up at Kujo. "I think he's found himself a mate."

Kujo frowned. "She's a wolf."

Six romped in the shadows with the wolf for a few minutes then ran back to the porch where Kujo and Molly stood.

Kujo knelt beside the dog and rubbed behind his ears. "Is that where you've been?"

Six pushed his nose against Kujo's hand.

Kujo laughed. "I guess we'd better get a bigger bag of dog food. Six is in love."

Six ran back to the wolf, and they disappeared into the darkness.

"Do you think he'll come back?" Kujo asked.

Molly nodded. "He will. We're part of his pack."

Kujo pulled her up against him and bent to kiss her.

She leaned into him. "Thank you for the best Christmas present ever."

"I love you, Molly. I believe you've given me the best Christmas surprise—and it wasn't the red dress." He laughed. "Although that would be right up there as second best. You're an amazing woman. I'm blessed to have you as my partner, my lover and my wife. Now, you're going to be the mother of our children." He held her close, his face buried in her hair.

"A baby and Six's return..." Molly laughed. "It'll be hard to top this Christmas."

"Yes, it will. But our baby will need a sibling..."

Molly shook her head. "Let's focus on one child at a time. And one litter of wolf puppies at a time."

She took his hand in hers and led him into the house.

All was right with their world.

No. All was perfect. It couldn't possibly get better.

Well, maybe it could.

As they passed through the living room to the bedroom, Kujo reached for the small of her back. "Where did you say that zipper was?"

CHAPTER 9

EARLY SPRING

"Kujo." As she stood in her slippers on the front porch of their cabin, Molly rubbed her small baby bump. "Kujo?" she called out louder.

Kujo slipped up behind her and covered her hands with his over her tummy. "Yeah, baby?"

She sighed. "I'm worried about Six."

He chuckled. "Six is fine."

"How do you know that? I haven't seen him in days. And he usually comes back every other day to eat."

Kujo nuzzled her neck. "He'll be back."

"And I haven't seen the white wolf in at least two months." Molly leaned back against her husband. "Do you think something happened to them?"

"She's probably nursing babies."

Molly's gaze shot up to Kujo's. "You think so? Isn't it a little soon?"

Again, Kujo laughed. "The canine gestation period is around sixty days. That was two months ago."

Molly turned to face him and wrapped her arms around his middle. "I hope Six is all right, and that the babies are healthy and safe."

Kujo smoothed a strand of her hair back from her forehead and pressed a kiss to her skin. "I'm sure they are."

"I guess, I'm missing Six," Moly said and leaned her forehead against his chest. "I hope they're all okay. With the ranchers angry about wolves taking their livestock, I'm afraid they'll shoot anything that looks like a wolf, including Six."

Kujo raised her chin and brushed his thumb across her bottom lip. "You can't worry about him."

She gave him a weak smile. "I can't help it. Six is family." The sound of tires on gravel and the roar of an engine made Molly glance over her shoulder.

A big, black truck rumbled along the gravel path leading up to Molly and Kujo's cabin.

Kujo frowned. "It's Hank."

"Can you tell if Sadie's with him?" Molly asked, smoothing a hand over her hair. Thankfully, she'd brushed it that morning, but she wasn't wearing a stitch of makeup. Her work with the FBI over the past few months had been done from her home office. She didn't have to wear a suit or makeup. Not that Sadie cared if Molly wore makeup. It was just that Sadie always looked like a star, no matter what she wore or didn't wear.

Molly was glad they were friends, or she'd have to be jealous of the woman. She pasted a smile on her face and waited for the truck to come to a halt. It was always good to see the Pattersons.

KUJO SHADED his eyes with a hand and squinted at the approaching truck. "Someone tall and blond is in there with him. Looks like Swede." As the truck pulled up in front of the house, Kujo dropped his hand and went to greet the men as Hank and Swede dropped down out of the truck. "Come to visit?" He held out his hand.

Hank took it and stared into Kujo's eyes. "I was at the feed store today and heard Martin Franklin say he'd shot a wolf attacking one of his spring calves."

Kujo stiffened, his hand freezing in mid-shake. "Yeah?"

Hank's lips pressed into a thin line. "A white one."

A gasp sounded behind Kujo, and Molly joined him. He slipped his arm around her. "We don't know that it was Six's mate," Kujo murmured, his hand tightening on her hip.

"Surely, there are other white wolves are in this area, aren't there?" Molly turned to Hank. "Did they say whether or not they saw Six with her?"

"I'm sorry." Hank shook his head. "He said the white female was alone. No sign of Six."

Molly nodded. "At least, they didn't shoot him." She looked up at Kujo. "We need to go look for him."

Kujo shook his head. "He could be anywhere."

"But we can't sit back and do nothing." Molly flung her arm in the air. "If they shot the mother, there are pups out there with no one to protect them." She pulled away from Kujo and paced across the ground. "We can go to where they shot the white wolf and backtrack from there."

"What's this *we?*" Kujo shook his head. "*You're* not going anywhere."

"But I can't sit around and do nothing," she said.

"You're pregnant," Kujo pointed out, and then winced. He always made her mad when he used her pregnancy as an excuse for her not to do something.

Molly propped her fists on her hips, her eyes flashing. "I'm pregnant, not an invalid."

Hank chuckled. "Molly, I know you're an FBI agent and tough as nails, but Kujo has a point. Tromping around in wolf territory isn't wise in your condition. Sadie told me how hard it was for you to get pregnant in the first place. I'd hate for you to compromise yours or the baby's health."

Molly's shoulders stiffened, and her brow descended.

For a moment, Kujo thought she would argue the point. He held his breath.

Finally, Molly huffed. "I hate it when you make a good point." She pointed a finger at Kujo. "But you're not pregnant."

He laughed and held up his hands. "No, thank goodness. And I'll get right out there and check the location of the kill."

"We'll go with you," Swede said. The tall, blond man, who could have been a Viking several centuries ago, grinned. "Maybe we should leave you with Sadie while we're gone," he suggested.

Molly shook her head. "I'm staying here in case Six comes home. I don't want to miss him. If they killed his mate, he might come home."

Kujo nodded. "True. All the more reason for you to stay put." He took her hand. "Will you be all right?"

Her chin lifted. "I can take care of myself."

"You're right. I know that." Kujo loved that about her. Molly was a badass FBI agent who could shoot as well as he could. But she was all soft and feminine when they were alone in their bedroom. He kissed the tip of her nose. "I still worry about you."

"Well, quit," she said, softening her words with a gentle smile. "Go find Six."

"You can ride with us." Hank faced Molly. "We'll be back before dark."

"I'll be here," she said. "And I'll let you know if I see Six before you return."

"We won't have cellphone reception out on Franklin's ranch," Hank warned.

"I'll text so you can read it when you can get reception," she said.

Kujo kissed her soundly then climbed into the backseat of Hank's truck.

For the next several hours, they drove around the Franklin's ranch and the nearby hills, searching for Six and the white female wolf's pups.

Martin Franklin showed them where he'd shot the wolf. "I know I hit it," he said. "I could tell the way it jerked and then limped away."

After looking around for a few minutes, they found a trail of blood.

Kujo hated that it could have been Six's mate. Based on the amount of blood, the wolf might have been fatally wounded. His heart hurt for his furry friend. The question was where she'd stashed the pups and whether Six was taking care of them.

After five hours of searching, Hank, Swede and Kujo headed into the little town of Eagle Rock and back out to Kujo's cabin.

Molly was waiting on the cabin's covered porch, wearing a thick jacket to ward off the cool mountain air. As soon as Kujo climbed out of the truck, Molly was there, wrapping her arms around his waist. "Thank you," she said.

"For what?" he asked, smoothing a hand over her hair. "We didn't find him."

"For trying." Molly turned a watery smile toward Hank and Swede. "Thank you."

Hank dipped his head. "We'd better get back. If we show up after dark, Sadie and Allie will be worried."

"We'll let you know if he comes back to the cabin." Molly waved at the two men who climbed into Hank's truck and headed for the White Oak Ranch.

For several minutes, Kujo stood with Molly on the porch, staring out at the mountains. "He'll come home."

"If he can," she whispered softly, her hand

resting lightly on her belly. "I worry about him and the pups."

"The pups would be old enough they wouldn't have to nurse," Kujo said.

Molly nodded. "But not old enough to hunt for themselves."

Kujo wrapped his arms around Molly's waist and pulled her back against his front. "You're going to make a great mother." He nuzzled the curve of her neck and kissed her there.

"Because I'm worried about Six's puppies?" Molly snorted softly. "I have to admit, my dreams are getting a little weird. I dreamed I had a litter."

"Of babies?"

She shook her head. "Of little white puppies."

He chuckled. "No more chocolate milk for you before bedtime."

She leaned back against him. "I'm worried about Six and those babies."

"I'm worried about you worrying." He turned her in his arms, tipped her chin up and brushed her lips with his. "We should call it a night. You need to get some rest."

She sighed and laid her cheek against his

chest. "I know you're right. You don't know how much I wanted to be out there with you and the guys today. I get frustrated when I'm held back."

"I know."

"But I also remember how hard it was to get pregnant." She laid a hand on her tiny bump. "I don't want anything to happen to our child."

He laid his hand over hers on her belly. "I love you, Molly. And I can't wait to meet our baby. Come on. Let's get you some supper, and I'll rub your back."

"Mmm. That sounds nice." She glanced once more over her shoulder.

"Don't worry," Kujo said. "Six knows where we live. He'll come back if he needs food or help."

"I hope so." Molly led the way back into the house.

Kujo stopped as he crossed the threshold. "You know, I'm going to check the barn."

Molly smiled. "I left the barn door open in case Six comes in at night. He'll have a warm dry place to sleep in the hay."

"Good." He grinned. "Glad we think alike."

She cupped his cheek. "It's one of the things I like best about you." Her brow dipped. "You might check anyway to make sure it didn't blow shut." She tilted her head. "For that matter, I'll go with you."

"You're supposed to be resting."

"I'm pregnant, and I'm past morning sickness." She hooked her hand through his elbow. "Let's do this. Then you promised me a backrub. You're not trying to get out of that, are you?"

"Never." He grinned and winked. "Your back is one of the things I like best about you."

The small wooden barn behind the cabin housed two four-wheelers and tools. They didn't have livestock, nor did they want any. The only animal they'd wanted around was Six.

The door to the barn stood open just enough that a dog Six's size could get through it.

Already, dusk had settled in on the hillside, the sun having gone below the mountain ridge above the cabin.

As he pushed the door wide, Kujo reached inside and flipped on the light switch.

A menacing growl echoed off the walls.

Molly's grip on Kujo's arm tightened. "Did you hear that?"

"I did," he said softly. "Get behind the door," he ordered.

"But—"

Kujo's jaw tightened. "Do it." He pushed her gently behind him and through the door, pulling his handgun from the shoulder holster he wore beneath his leather jacket.

Molly ducked back out of the barn and around the heavy door. "Be careful," she called out.

Another growl sounded low and urgent.

Kujo searched the interior of the barn, focusing on every dark, shadowy corner. "Six," he called out, using his commanding voice. "Come."

The growling ceased, followed by a long, eerie silence.

Then out of the shadows, Six emerged, his teeth bared in a threatening snarl.

Kujo stood tall, his jaw hardening. "Come." He pointed to the ground beside him. The same position Six used to assume when he'd been the highly trained Military Working Dog that had been decorated for his bravery in the line of duty.

Six stood for a moment longer, snarling. Then he lifted his nose and sniffed the air. The hackles on the back of his neck lowered, and he trotted over to sit at Kujo's feet. The animal stared up at him, his tongue hanging down, his mouth open as if he were giving his trainer a happy grin.

Kujo knelt beside Six and wrapped his arms around the dog. "Hey, buddy. You're a sight for sore eyes."

Kujo leaned against his leg for a moment then trotted back to the stack of hay he'd been hiding behind and disappeared into the shadows again.

"It's okay," Kujo called out to the dog.

"Can I come in?" Molly asked.

"No," he responded automatically. Then he thought again. "I mean, yeah."

Molly poked her head around the door, her eyes wide and hopeful. "Is it Six?"

"Yes, it is." Kujo held out his hand.

Molly placed her fingers in his palm. "Where is he?"

Kujo tilted his head toward the bales. "Behind that stack of hay."

"Six?" Molly called out.

The German Shepherd stuck his head around the side of a bale.

Molly's smile spread across her face. "Oh, Six." She started forward. "Come here, sweetie."

A ghost of a movement made Kujo grab her arm and pull her back against him. "Don't move."

"But it's Six," she said.

"We need to back out of this barn slowly." Kujo's grip on her arm tightened. "Trust me on this, Molly."

Molly glanced at Six's head, a frown creasing her forehead. "Okay, but I don't see why we're being so—" A movement beside Six made Molly gasp.

A large white head appeared beside Six and startlingly, blue eyes peered out at them. As she limped another step forward, a dark red streak of blood appeared on her right shoulder. The female wolf bared her teeth and gave a low, rumbling growl.

The sound raised the hair on the back of Kujo's neck.

Six stepped out from behind the bale, placing himself between the mother wolf, Kujo and Molly.

Kujo held his handgun in front of him, unwilling to shoot with Six in his direct line of fire, but ready in case the wolf attacked Molly. "Leave the barn, Molly. Move slowly and don't turn your back."

The wolf growled again.

Molly slowly moved backward toward the barn door. "What about you?" she murmured.

"I'm armed."

"But you can't shoot her. She has babies to feed and she's wounded."

"It's up to her. If she makes a move on either one of us..." Kujo didn't like the thought of shooting the mother wolf but had to think of his own family and the baby Molly carried inside.

"So, she was the white wolf the rancher shot," Molly said. "But where are her pups?" She was almost to the door when a white fuzzy creature scrambled out from behind the bale and ran toward Six.

Mama wolf snatched him up by the scruff of the neck and deposited him back behind the hay.

A darker pup shot out past its mother and raced for Six, crashing into his legs.

Molly laughed and clapped a hand over her mouth. "That one looks like Six," she said.

"Maybe so," Kujo said, "but the pups are half wolf."

"Don't worry, I'm not going to try to keep them," Molly said from the door to the barn. "We need to leave them alone and let Six and his mate care for them. I'm just happy to know the babies are all right. But I'm worried about the mother."

Kujo backed away from Six and the wolf, until he slipped out of the barn with Molly.

He left the door open just enough for the animals to come and go easily.

Molly stood outside in the moonlight, her gaze on the barn. "I'm glad they decided to stay here." She frowned. "It's okay, isn't it?"

"As long as they don't threaten you or me." Kujo held his gun in his hand in case the wolf got past Six and went for Molly.

"I'd rather they were here than being shot at again by some rancher," Molly said, leaning into Kujo.

"I'm glad they're here as well." His arm tightened around her. "I'd like to get a vet to take a look at the wolf."

Molly snorted. "Like she would let that happen."

"The US Fish and Wildlife service might be able to help. Even if they have to tranquilize her."

Molly sighed. "You're right. The only way they'll get her is to tranquilize her. If she's hurt badly enough, she might not be able to return to the wild. She'll need a forever home in a wolf sanctuary."

"No matter what happens to her, the pups will need to move them to a wolf sanctuary."

Molly's brow furrowed. "Can't they stay and live in the mountains like their mother's pack?"

Kujo shook his head. "They're only half wolf. Their domestic genes could hold them back from fending for and feeding themselves. And the wolf pack might shun them. Wolves rely on their pack to protect and care for their young. Alone, they have less chance of surviving in the wild."

Molly's lips twisted. "I think I've read something to that extent. It'll be a challenge to catch them."

"We aren't going to catch them. We'll have the fish and wildlife folks trap them and move them to a safe location where they can be cared for." Kujo slid his spare hand around her waist and pulled her close. "In the meantime, you probably shouldn't visit the barn."

Molly nodded. "Agreed. Neither one of us should."

Kujo led Molly back to the house, where he

called Hank Patterson to let him know they'd found Six and the situation. He placed the call on speaker so Molly could listen as well.

"I'll notify the US Fish and Wildlife right away. I also know of a wolf sanctuary in Wyoming," Hank said. "I'll give them a call in the morning and give them a heads-up. You two going to be all right?"

Kujo nodded, even though Hank couldn't see him make the gesture. "Knowing Six and his mate are safe for now makes us feel a whole lot better."

"When the mother and the pups are moved, do you think Six will return home for good?" Hank asked.

"I hope so. He's not cut out for the wild life." Kujo glanced across at Molly. "Neither are we. Not with a kid on the way." He held out his hand for Molly's.

She curled her fingers around his. "Speaking of kids..." Molly grinned at Kujo. "We look forward to babysitting on Friday, so you and Sadie can have your date night. Thanks for thinking of us."

Hank chuckled. "It was my idea. Sadie says

I'm being sadistic for wanting Kujo to have to change diapers."

Kujo frowned. "I agree with Sadie on this one."

Molly playfully slapped Kujo's arm. "He needs the practice. Joseph promised that when our baby comes, he's going to be a hands-on kind of dad." Her lips spread in a wide smile. "There's nothing more hands-on than changing a dirty diaper."

"He'll handle it like a pro," Hank predicted. "Like anything else he's ever attempted."

His lips twisting into a wry smile, Kujo brought Molly's hand up and pressed a kiss to the backs of her knuckles. "Glad you have confidence in me to take care of your children."

"Oh, I don't," Hank admitted. "But you'll have Molly to help. Between you two, you'll manage."

After Hank ended the call, Kujo took Molly into his arms. "Feel better knowing where the rest of our little family is?"

She leaned against him, resting her hand on his chest. "I do. Thank you for going the extra mile to find Six."

"He's one of our pack. I would do no less,"

Kujo said. "Now that he's back, I can concentrate on other, more important matters." He pulled her close and tipped up her chin. "Like kissing my beautiful wife."

"I like the way you think," she said and stood on her toes to give back as good as she got.

A moment later, Kujo scooped her up in his arms and carried her to their little bedroom with the four-poster bed and the down comforter. They wouldn't need it's warmth for a while. They always managed to make it hot in their bedroom, enjoying the cool night air on their naked skin after making passionate love.

Later that night, they pulled the comforter up over their bodies and snuggled close.

"I love you, Joseph Kuntz," Molly said into the darkness. "I can't imagine loving anyone as much as I love you." She smoothed a hand over his naked chest. "Do you think I can love a baby as much?"

He covered her hand with his. "That's the beauty of love. Our hearts can expand to include each other and any little guys who come along."

"Or girls," Molly corrected.

"Or girls. Especially if they're as pretty as

their mama." He kissed the tip of her nose and claimed her lips in a long, toe-curling kiss. "I love you, Molly, and I can't wait for our baby to come into the world. It'll be a part of you and me, making our lives even more complete. I'm thankful for the day Six found you in the mountains."

"Me, too," she said. "He saved my life."

"And by so doing, you and Six saved mine." He held Molly close until her breathing became deep and regular.

He was forever in Six's debt for bringing Molly into his life. She completed him.

THE END

Thank you for reading Dog Days of Christmas. Follow Kujo and Six as they travel to Colorado to set up another branch of the Brotherhood Protectors in SEAL Salvation.

About SEAL Salvation:

All he wants is to be left alone

Jake Cogburn lost his leg, his career, his

brotherhood and his will to live when he stepped on that IED in Afghanistan. Back in his home state of Colorado, he's determined to bury himself as deeply as he can in a bottle of Jack Daniels until the pain in his leg and his heart is so numb he can no longer feel.

No man left behind

Hank Patterson refuses to let his buddy, Jake, slowly kill himself with alcohol. Hank's plan to expand the Brotherhood Protectors into Colorado will only work if he can hire the best men for the job. He wants Jake and sends fellow Coloradan, Kujo, to pull Jake out of an alcohol-induced haze to work for the team. Hank's contact has a place they can set up operations while flying under the radar—a flailing dude ranch, run by a former Marine Gunnery sergeant and his feisty daughter.

Rucker Tate is as unconventional as the name her father gave her upon her birth. After her mother died when Rucker was only a baby, she was left in the capable hands of her taciturn Marine father to be raised tough and ready to accept any challenge. Including adopting a Military Working Dog with only three legs.

Retraining the dog to live in a civilian world is practically a full time job. She's up for it, until she witnesses a meeting she shouldn't have seen and is thrown into the path of a killer who wants to wipe her memory, by erasing her from existence.

Jake's first assignment as a Brotherhood Protector is to stick to the rebellious daughter of the owner of a dude ranch and make certain she doesn't fall victim to the person gunning for her. Meanwhile, Rucker fights to keep from falling victim to the love blossoming in her heart over the young Navy SEAL who dogs her every footstep. Even her German Shepherd likes the SEAL better than Rucker. And worse...she finds herself falling for the cranky, one-legged frogman. Her challenge is to live long enough to see where these feelings take her.

BROTHERHOOD PROTECTORS: Fighting men, chosen for their skills, recommended by their peers and trained to protect, guard, extract and rescue, these men are the elite, the strong and perfect for their civilian assignments. Former military, special opera-

tions men, use their combat and intelligence skills to assist those in need. Brotherhood Protectors, the brainchild of Hank Patterson in Montana, has set up operations in the mountains of Colorado.

BREAKING SILENCE

DELTA FORCE STRONG BOOK #1

ELLE JAMES

New York Times & USA Today
Bestselling Author

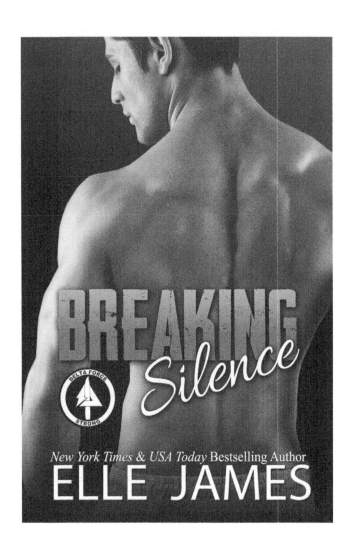

BREAKING Silence

New York Times & USA Today Bestselling Author

ELLE JAMES

SEAL Salvation

CHAPTER 1

HAD he known they would be deployed so soon after their last short mission to El Salvador, Rucker Sloan wouldn't have bought that dirt bike from his friend Duff. Now, it would sit there for months before he actually got to take it out to the track.

The team had been given forty-eight hours to pack their shit, take care of business and get onto the C130 that would transport them to Afghanistan.

Now, boots on the ground, duffel bags stowed in their assigned quarters behind the wire, they were ready to take on any mission the powers that be saw fit to assign.

What he wanted most that morning, after

being awake for the past thirty-six hours, was a cup of strong, black coffee.

The rest of his team had hit the sack as soon as they got in. Rucker had already met with their commanding officer, gotten a brief introduction to the regional issues and had been told to get some rest. They'd be operational within the next forty-eight hours.

Too wound up to sleep, Rucker followed a stream of people he hoped were heading for the chow hall. He should be able to get coffee there.

On the way, he passed a sand volleyball court where two teams played against each other. One of the teams had four players, the other only three. The four-person squad slammed a ball to the ground on the other side of the net. The only female player ran after it as it rolled toward Rucker.

He stopped the ball with his foot and picked it up.

The woman was tall, slender, blond-haired and blue-eyed. She wore an Army PT uniform of shorts and an Army T-shirt with her hair secured back from her face in a ponytail seated on the crown of her head.

Without makeup, and sporting a sheen of

perspiration, she was sexy as hell, and the men on both teams knew it.

They groaned when Rucker handed her the ball. He'd robbed them of watching the female soldier bending over to retrieve the runaway.

She took the ball and frowned. "Do you play?"

"I have," he answered.

"We could use a fourth." She lifted her chin in challenge.

Tired from being awake for the past thirty-six hours, Rucker opened his mouth to say *hell no*. But he made the mistake of looking into her sky-blue eyes and instead said, "I'm in."

What the hell was he thinking?

Well, hadn't he been wound up from too many hours sitting in transit? What he needed was a little physical activity to relax his mind and muscles. At least, that's what he told himself in the split-second it took to step into the sandbox and serve up a heaping helping of whoop-ass.

He served six times before the team playing opposite finally returned one. In between each serve, his side gave him high-fives, all members except one—the blonde with the blue eyes he stood behind, admiring the length of her legs beneath her black Army PT shorts.

Twenty minutes later, Rucker's team won the match. The teams broke up and scattered to get showers or breakfast in the chow hall.

"Can I buy you a cup of coffee?" the pretty blonde asked.

"Only if you tell me your name." He twisted his lips into a wry grin. "I'd like to know who delivered those wicked spikes."

She held out her hand. "Nora Michaels," she said.

He gripped her hand in his, pleased to feel firm pressure. Women might be the weaker sex, but he didn't like a dead fish handshake from males or females. Firm and confident was what he preferred. Like her ass in those shorts.

She cocked an eyebrow. "And you are?"

He'd been so intent thinking about her legs and ass, he'd forgotten to introduce himself. "Rucker Sloan. Just got in less than an hour ago."

"Then you could probably use a tour guide to the nearest coffee."

He nodded. "Running on fumes here. Good coffee will help."

"I don't know about good, but it's coffee and it's fresh." She released his hand and fell in step beside him, heading in the direction of some of the others from their volleyball game.

"As long as it's strong and black, I'll be happy."

She laughed. "And awake for the next twenty-four hours."

"Spoken from experience?" he asked, casting a glance in her direction.

She nodded. "I work nights in the medical facility. It can be really boring and hard to stay awake when we don't have any patients to look after." She held up her hands. "Not that I want any of our boys injured and in need of our care."

"But it does get boring," he guessed.

"It makes for a long deployment." She held out her hand. "Nice to meet you, Rucker. Is Rucker a call sign or your real name?"

He grinned. "Real name. That was the only thing my father gave me before he cut out and left my mother and me to make it on our own."

"Your mother raised you, and you still joined the Army?" She raised an eyebrow. "Most mothers don't want their boys to go off to war."

"It was that or join a gang and end up dead in a gutter," he said. "She couldn't afford to send me to college. I was headed down the gang path when she gave me the ultimatum. Join and get the GI-Bill, or she would cut me off and I'd be out in the streets. To her, it was the only way to get me out of L.A. and to have the potential to go to college someday."

She smiled "And you stayed in the military."

He nodded. "I found a brotherhood that was better than any gang membership in LA. For now, I take college classes online. It was my mother's dream for me to graduate college. She never went, and she wanted so much more for me than the streets of L.A.. When my gig is up with the Army, if I haven't finished my degree, I'll go to college fulltime."

"And major in what?" Nora asked.

"Business management. I'm going to own my own security service. I want to put my combat skills to use helping people who need dedicated and specialized protection."

Nora nodded. "Sounds like a good plan."

"I know the protection side of things. I need to learn the business side and business law. Life will be different on the civilian side."

"True."

"How about you? What made you sign up?" he asked.

She shrugged. "I wanted to put my nursing

degree to good use and help our men and women in uniform. This is my first assignment after training."

"Drinking from the firehose?" Rucker stopped in front of the door to the mess hall.

She nodded. "Yes. But it's the best baptism under fire medical personnel can get. I'll be a better nurse for it when I return to the States."

"How much longer do you have to go?" he asked, hoping that she'd say she'd be there as long as he was. In his case, he never knew how long their deployments would last. One week, one month, six months...

She gave him a lopsided smile. "I ship out in a week."

"That's too bad." He opened the door for her. "I just got here. That doesn't give us much time to get to know each other."

"That's just as well." Nora stepped through the door. "I don't want to be accused of fraternizing. I'm too close to going back to spoil my record."

Rucker chuckled. "Playing volleyball and sharing a table while drinking coffee won't get you written up. I like the way you play. I'm curious to know where you learned to spike like that."

"I guess that's reasonable. Coffee first." She led him into the chow hall.

The smells of food and coffee made Rucker's mouth water.

He grabbed a tray and loaded his plate with eggs, toast and pancakes drenched in syrup. Last, he stopped at the coffee urn and filled his cup with freshly brewed black coffee.

When he looked around, he found Nora seated at one of the tables, holding a mug in her hands, a small plate with cottage cheese and peaches on it.

He strode over to her. "Mind if I join you?"

"As long as you don't hit on me," she said with cocked eyebrows.

"You say that as if you've been hit on before."

She nodded and sipped her steaming brew. "I lost count how many times in the first week I was here."

"Shows they have good taste in women and, unfortunately, limited manners."

"And you're better?" she asked, a smile twitching the corners of her lips.

"I'm not hitting on you. You can tell me to

leave, and I'll be out of this chair so fast, you won't have time to enunciate the V."

She stared straight into his eyes, canted her head to one side and said, "Leave."

In the middle of cutting into one of his pancakes, Rucker dropped his knife and fork on the tray, shot out of his chair and left with his tray, sloshing coffee as he moved. He hoped she was just testing him. If she wasn't...oh, well. He was used to eating meals alone. If she was, she'd have to come to him.

He took a seat at the next table, his back to her, and resumed cutting into his pancake.

Nora didn't utter a word behind him.

Oh, well. He popped a bite of syrupy sweet pancake in his mouth and chewed thoughtfully. She was only there for another week. Man, she had a nice ass...and those legs... He sighed and bent over his plate to stab his fork into a sausage link.

"This chair taken?" a soft, female voice sounded in front of him.

He looked up to see the pretty blond nurse standing there with her tray in her hands, a crooked smile on her face.

He lifted his chin in silent acknowledgement.

She laid her tray on the table and settled onto the chair. "I didn't think you'd do it."

"Fair enough. You don't know me," he said.

"I know that you joined the Army to get out of street life. That your mother raised you after your father skipped out, that you're working toward a business degree and that your name is Rucker." She sipped her coffee.

He nodded, secretly pleased she'd remembered all that. Maybe there was hope for getting to know the pretty nurse before she redeployed to the States. And who knew? They might run into each other on the other side of the pond.

Still, he couldn't show too much interest, or he'd be no better than the other guys who'd hit on her. "Since you're redeploying back to the States in a week, and I'm due to go out on a mission, probably within the next twenty-four to forty-eight hours, I don't know if it's worth our time to get to know each other any more than we already have."

She nodded. "I guess that's why I want to sit with you. You're not a danger to my perfect record of no fraternizing. I don't have to worry that you'll fall in love with me in such a short amount of time." She winked.

He chuckled. "As I'm sure half of this base has fallen in love with you since you've been here."

She shrugged. "I don't know if it's love, but it's damned annoying."

"How so?"

She rolled her eyes toward the ceiling. "I get flowers left on my door every day."

"And that's annoying? I'm sure it's not easy coming up with flowers out here in the desert." He set down his fork and took up his coffee mug. "I think it's sweet." He held back a smile. Well, almost.

"They're hand-drawn on notepad paper and left on the door of my quarters and on the door to the shower tent." She shook her head. "It's kind of creepy and stalkerish."

Rucker nodded. "I see your point. The guys should at least have tried their hands at origami flowers, since the real things are scarce around here."

Nora smiled. "I'm not worried about the pictures, but the line for sick call is ridiculous."

"How so?"

"So many of the guys come up with the lamest excuses to come in and hit on me. I asked to work the nightshift to avoid sick call altogether."

"You have a fan group." He smiled. "Has the adoration gone to your head?"

She snorted softly. "No."

"You didn't get this kind of reaction back in the States?"

"I haven't been on active duty for long. I only decided to join the Army after my mother passed away. I was her fulltime nurse for a couple years as she went through stage four breast cancer. We thought she might make it." Her shoulders sagged. "But she didn't."

"I'm sorry to hear that. My mother meant a lot to me, as well. I sent money home every month after I enlisted and kept sending it up until the day she died suddenly of an aneurysm."

"I'm so sorry about your mother's passing," Nora said, shaking her head. "Wow. As an enlisted man, how did you make enough to send some home?"

"I ate in the chow hall and lived on post. I didn't party or spend money on civilian clothes or booze. Mom needed it. I gave it to her."

"You were a good son to her," Nora said.

His chest tightened. "She died of an aneurysm

a couple of weeks before she was due to move to Texas where I'd purchased a house for her."

"Wow. And, let me guess, you blame yourself for not getting her to Texas sooner...?" Her gaze captured his.

Her words hit home, and he winced. "Yeah. I should've done it sooner."

"Can't bring people back with regrets." Nora stared into her coffee cup. "I learned that. The only thing I could do was move forward and get on with living. I wanted to get away from Milwaukee and the home I'd shared with my mother. Not knowing where else to go, I wandered past a realtor's office and stepped into a recruiter's office. I had my nursing degree, they wanted and needed nurses on active duty. I signed up, they put me through some officer training and here I am." She held her arms out.

"Playing volleyball in Afghanistan, working on your tan during the day and helping soldiers at night." Rucker gave her a brief smile. "I, for one, appreciate what you're doing for our guys and gals."

"I do the best I can," she said softly. "I just wish I could do more. I'd rather stay here than redeploy back to the States, but they're afraid if they keep us here too long, we'll burn out or get PTSD."

"One week, huh?"

She nodded. "One week."

"In my field, one week to redeploy back to the States is a dangerous time. Anything can happen and usually does."

"Yeah, but you guys are on the frontlines, if not behind enemy lines. I'm back here. What could happen?"

Rucker flinched. "Oh, sweetheart, you didn't just say that..." He glanced around, hoping no one heard her tempt fate with those dreaded words *What could happen?*

Nora grinned. "You're not superstitious, are you?"

"In what we do, we can't afford not to be," he said, tossing salt over his shoulder.

"I'll be fine," she said in a reassuring, nurse's voice.

"Stop," he said, holding up his hand. "You're only digging the hole deeper." He tossed more salt over his other shoulder.

Nora laughed.

"Don't laugh." He handed her the saltshaker. "Do it."

"I'm not tossing salt over my shoulder. Someone has to clean the mess hall."

Rucker leaned close and shook salt over her shoulder. "I don't know if it counts if someone else throws salt over your shoulder, but I figure you now need every bit of luck you can get."

"You're a fighter but afraid of a little bad luck." Nora shook her head. "Those two things don't seem to go together."

"You'd be surprised how easily my guys are freaked by the littlest things."

"And you," she reminded him.

"You asking *what could happen?* isn't a little thing. That's in-your-face tempting fate." Rucker was laying it on thick to keep her grinning, but deep down, he believed what he was saying. And it didn't make a difference the amount of education he had or the statistics that predicted outcomes. His gut told him she'd just tempted fate with her statement. Maybe he was over-thinking things. Now, he was worried she wouldn't make it back to the States alive.

NORA LIKED RUCKER. He was the first guy who'd walked away without an argument since she'd arrived at the base in Afghanistan. He'd meant what he'd said and proved it. His dark brown hair and deep green eyes, coupled with broad shoulders and a narrow waist, made him even more attractive. Not all the men were in as good a shape as Rucker. And he seemed to have a very determined attitude.

She hadn't known what to expect when she'd deployed. Being the center of attention of almost every single male on the base hadn't been one of her expectations. She'd only ever considered herself average in the looks department. But when the men outnumbered women by more than ten to one, she guessed average appearance moved up in the ranks.

"Where did you learn to play volleyball?" Rucker asked, changing the subject of her leaving and her flippant comment about what could happen in one week.

"I was on the volleyball team in high school. It got me a scholarship to a small university in my home state of Minnesota, where I got my Bachelor of Science degree in Nursing."

"It takes someone special to be a nurse," he

stated. "Is that what you always wanted to be?"

She shook her head. "I wanted to be a fire-fighter when I was in high school."

"What made you change your mind?"

She stared down at the coffee growing cold in her mug. "My mother was diagnosed with cancer when I was a senior in high school. I wanted to help but felt like I didn't know enough to be of assistance." She looked up. "She made it through chemo and radiation treatments and still came to all of my volleyball games. I thought she was in the clear."

"She wasn't?" Rucker asked, his tone low and gentle.

"She didn't tell me any different. When I got the scholarship, I told her I wanted to stay close to home to be with her. She insisted I go and play volleyball for the university. I was pretty good and played for the first two years I was there. I quit the team in my third year to start the nursing program. I didn't know there was anything wrong back home. I called every week to talk to Mom. She never let on that she was sick." She forced a smile. "But you don't want my sob story. You probably want to know what's going on around here."

He set his mug on the table. "If we were alone in a coffee bar back in the States, I'd reach across the table and take your hand."

"Oh, please. Don't do that." She looked around the mess hall, half expecting someone might have overheard Rucker's comment. "You're enlisted. I'm an officer. That would get us into a whole lot of trouble."

"Yeah, but we're also two human beings. I wouldn't be human if I didn't feel empathy for you and want to provide comfort."

She set her coffee cup on the table and laid her hands in her lap. "I'll be satisfied with the thought. Thank you."

"Doesn't seem like enough. When did you find out your mother was sick?"

She swallowed the sadness that welled in her throat every time she remembered coming home to find out her mother had been keeping her illness from her. "It wasn't until I went home for Christmas in my senior year that I realized she'd been lying to me for a while." She laughed in lieu of sobbing. "I don't care who they are, old people don't always tell the truth."

"How long had she been keeping her sickness from you?"

"She'd known the cancer had returned halfway through my junior year. I hadn't gone home that summer because I'd been working hard to get my coursework and clinical hours in the nursing program. When I went home at Christmas…" Nora gulped. "She wasn't the same person. She'd lost so much weight and looked twenty years older."

"Did you stay home that last semester?" Rucker asked.

"Mom insisted I go back to school and finish what I'd started. Like your mother, she hadn't gone to college. She wanted her only child to graduate. She was afraid that if I stayed home to take care of her, I wouldn't finish my nursing degree."

"I heard from a buddy of mine that those programs can be hard to get into," he said. "I can see why she wouldn't want you to drop everything in your life to take care of her."

Nora gave him a watery smile. "That's what she said. As soon as my last final was over, I returned to my hometown. I became her nurse. She lasted another three months before she slipped away."

"That's when you joined the Army?"

She shook her head. "Dad was so heartbroken, I stayed a few months until he was feeling better. I got a job at a local emergency room. On weekends, my father and I worked on cleaning out the house and getting it ready to put on the market."

"Is your dad still alive?" Rucker asked.

Nora nodded. "He lives in Texas. He moved to a small house with a big backyard." She forced a smile. "He has a garden, and all the ladies in his retirement community think he's the cat's meow. He still misses Mom, but he's getting on with his life."

Rucker tilted his head. "When did you join the military?"

"When Dad sold the house and moved into his retirement community. I worried about him, but he's doing better."

"And you?"

"I miss her. But she'd whip my ass if I wallowed in self-pity for more than a moment. She was a strong woman and expected me to be the same."

Rucker grinned. "From what I've seen, you are."

Nora gave him a skeptical look. "You've only

seen me playing volleyball. It's just a game." Not that she'd admit it, but she was a real softy when it came to caring for the sick and injured.

"If you're half as good at nursing, which I'm willing to bet you are, you're amazing." He started to reach across the table for her hand. Before he actually touched her, he grabbed the saltshaker and shook it over his cold breakfast.

"You just got in this morning?" Nora asked.

Rucker nodded.

"How long will you be here?" she asked.

"I don't know."

"What do you mean, you don't know? I thought when people were deployed, they were given a specific timeframe."

"Most people are. We're deployed where and when needed."

Nora frowned. "What are you? Some kind of special forces team?"

His lips pressed together. "Can't say."

She sat back. He was some kind of Special Forces. "Army, right?"

He nodded.

That would make him Delta Force. The elite of the elite. A very skilled soldier who undertook incredibly dangerous missions. She gulped and stopped herself from reaching across the table to take his hand. "Well, I hope all goes well while you and your team are here."

"Thanks."

A man hurried across the chow hall wearing shorts and an Army T-shirt. He headed directly toward their table.

Nora didn't recognize him. "Expecting someone?" she asked Rucker, tipping her head toward the man.

Rucker turned, a frown pulling his eyebrows together. "Why the hell's Dash awake?"

Nora frowned. "Dash? Please tell me that's his callsign, not his real name."

Rucker laughed. "It should be his real name. He's first into the fight, and he's fast." Rucker stood and faced his teammate. "What's up?"

"CO wants us all in the Tactical Operations Center," Dash said. "On the double."

"Guess that's my cue to exit." Rucker turned to Nora. "I enjoyed our talk."

She nodded. "Me, too."

Dash grinned. "Tell you what…I'll stay and finish your conversation while you see what the commander wants."

Rucker hooked Dash's arm twisted it up

behind his back, and gave him a shove toward the door. "You heard the CO, he wants all of us." Rucker winked at Nora. "I hope to see you on the volleyball court before you leave."

"Same. Good luck." Nora's gaze followed Rucker's broad shoulders and tight ass out of the chow hall. Too bad she'd only be there another week before she shipped out. She would've enjoyed more volleyball and coffee with the Delta Force operative.

He'd probably be on maneuvers that entire week.

She stacked her tray and coffee cup in the collection area and left the chow hall, heading for the building where she shared her quarters with Beth Drennan, a nurse she'd become friends with during their deployment together.

As close as they were, Nora didn't bring up her conversation with the Delta. With only a week left at the base, she probably wouldn't run into him again. Though she would like to see him again, she prayed he didn't end up in the hospital.

SEAL Salvation

ABOUT THE AUTHOR

ELLE JAMES also writing as MYLA JACKSON is a *New York Times* and *USA Today* Bestselling author of books including cowboys, intrigues and paranormal adventures that keep her readers on the edges of their seats. When she's not at her computer, she's traveling, snow skiing, boating, or riding her ATV, dreaming up new stories. Learn more about Elle James at www.elle-james.com

Website | Facebook | Twitter | GoodReads | Newsletter | BookBub | Amazon

Or visit her alter ego Myla Jackson at mylajackson.com
Website | Facebook | Twitter | Newsletter

Follow Me!
www.ellejames.com
ellejames@ellejames.com

ALSO BY ELLE JAMES

Warrior's Resolve (#5)

The Outrider Series

Homicide at Whiskey Gulch (#1)

Hideout at Whiskey Gulch (#2)

Hellfire Series

Hellfire, Texas (#1)

Justice Burning (#2)

Smoldering Desire (#3)

Hellfire in High Heels (#4)

Playing With Fire (#5)

Up in Flames (#6)

Total Meltdown (#7)

Take No Prisoners Series

SEAL's Honor (#1)

SEAL'S Desire (#2)

SEAL's Embrace (#3)

SEAL's Obsession (#4)

SEAL's Proposal (#5)

SEAL's Seduction (#6)

SEAL'S Defiance (#7)

SEAL's Deception (#8)

SEAL's Deliverance (#9)

SEAL's Ultimate Challenge (#10)

Billionaire Online Dating Service

The Billionaire Husband Test (#1)

The Billionaire Cinderella Test (#2)

The Billionaire Bride Test (#3)

The Billionaire Daddy Test (#4)

The Billionaire Matchmaker Test (#5)

The Billionaire Glitch Date (#6)

The Billionaire Perfect Date (#7) coming soon

The Billionaire Replacement Date (#8) coming soon

The Billionaire Wedding Date (#9) coming soon

Hearts & Heroes Series

Wyatt's War (#1)

Mack's Witness (#2)

Ronin's Return (#3)

Sam's Surrender (#4)

Cajun Magic Mystery Series

Voodoo on the Bayou (#1)

Voodoo for Two (#2)

Deja Voodoo (#3)

Cajun Magic Mysteries Books 1-3

Texas Billionaire Club

Tarzan & Janine (#1)

Something To Talk About (#2)

Who's Your Daddy (#3)

Love & War (#4)

Declan's Defenders

Marine Force Recon (#1)

Show of Force (#2)

Full Force (#3)

Driving Force (#4)

Tactical Force (#5)

Disruptive Force (#6)

Mission: Six

One Intrepid SEAL

Two Dauntless Hearts

Three Courageous Words

Four Relentless Days

Five Ways to Surrender

Six Minutes to Midnight

Thunder Horse Redemption (#3)

Christmas at Thunder Horse Ranch (#4)

Demon Series

Hot Demon Nights (#1)

Demon's Embrace (#2)

Tempting the Demon (#3)

Lords of the Underworld

Witch's Initiation (#1)

Witch's Seduction (#2)

The Witch's Desire (#3)

Possessing the Witch (#4)

Stealth Operations Specialists (SOS)

Nick of Time

Alaskan Fantasy

Boys Behaving Badly Anthology

Rogues (#1)

Blue Collar (#2)

Pirates (#3)

Stranded (#4)

First Responder (#5)

Blown Away

Warrior's Conquest

Enslaved by the Viking Short Story

Conquests

Smokin' Hot Firemen

Protecting the Colton Bride

Protecting the Colton Bride & Colton's Cowboy Code

Heir to Murder

Secret Service Rescue

High Octane Heroes

Haunted

Engaged with the Boss

Cowboy Brigade

Time Raiders: The Whisper

Bundle of Trouble

Killer Body

Operation XOXO

An Unexpected Clue

Baby Bling

Under Suspicion, With Child

Texas-Size Secrets

Cowboy Sanctuary

Lakota Baby

Dakota Meltdown

Beneath the Texas Moon